Granny Griggs's Pig

and other tales

Contents

Dedication

To

my parents, Jack and Dorothy,

my grandparents Reuben and Rose, Tom and Alice,

and all who went before them.

Introduction

I've always been interested in the past. It probably goes hand in hand with a tendency to prefer the ancient to the modern, at least in the realms of culture, language and music. As a child I would listen avidly to tales told by parents, grandparents and others. And I grew up with a love of history, largely instilled in me by a wild-haired, lovably crazy teacher called Arthur Lloyd.

In more recent years, as census, birth, marriage and death records became increasingly available on-line, I started doing some serious research to expand the knowledge I already had of my family history (and in the process met three second cousins engaged in the same activity – none of us had previously met or even knew of one another's existence).

The paternal half of my family tree centres around the town of Haverhill and the nearby village of Withersfield in the south-west corner of Suffolk, close to the borders with Essex and Cambridgeshire (indeed, Haverhill was for a time considered to be in Essex). Almost all the ancestors I have discovered on that side were born within a ten-mile radius of Haverhill, including villages in Suffolk (Kedington, Hundon, Great Wratting, Great Bradley, Poslingford), Essex (Sturmer, Helions Bumpstead and Steeple Bumpstead) and Cambridgeshire (Castle Camps, Shudy Camps, Bartlow and Linton).

The maternal half is quite different. My mother was born near the maritime town of Lymington on the edge of the New Forest. During the preceding century her father's family (the menfolk were mostly seamen) had moved to and fro between Lymington and the Isle of Wight and her mother's family were at Brockenhurst in the heart of the Forest but go back a few more generations and there are branches all over England – Hampshire, Sussex, Berkshire, Dorset, Staffordshire, County Durham, Northumberland and possible Norfolk.

As the data accumulated, the idea of a book began to form in my mind – and "lock-down" during the covid-19 pandemic provided a good opportunity to start putting it all together.

The book is divided into three main sections.

In the first two, **The Nunn Side** (father's family) and **The Murray Side** (mother's family), I have used a little imagination to embellish the bare facts as I know them and produce a collection of short stories. The characters in these stories are real people; even the "bit players" (e.g., the men in the pub) are names from the records of people who might conceivably have been there at the time.

The third section **Loose Ends** describes some areas of research which have presented me with a conundrum, are still "work in progress" or for whatever reason have not prompted a story but which I hope might be of some interest.

There are also some of my own childhood memories and a few general observations on genealogical research.

Obviously, I can't show you my full family tree here, not that I suppose many readers would be interested anyway. However, I have included a few charts showing the main lines of descent. The names in bold type are the characters whose stories I've told here.

There are also a few simple maps of places where the stories took place. I've tried to depict them as they might have been at the times those events took place and to mark any relevant buildings, roads and other features.

My ancestors were not famous people. One or two were respected members of their local community but most were ordinary, often illiterate, labourers and housewives. Their lives were often hard; some spent their last days in the workhouse. A few even found themselves on the wrong side of the law. But they all had a story to tell. If only I knew more of them…

The Nunn Side

In my father's house are many mansions

The Soldier's Confession

24th May 1828

John Wayman was reading the Norwich Mercury over breakfast when an article caught his eye. It began "The neighbourhood of Haverhill has been thrown into a state of great excitement, in consequence of intelligence having been received of a confession of murder, the scene of which is laid in that town…", but it was the name of Martin Cracknell that attracted his attention. He knew that name. How could he forget one of the strangest cases in his career as a coroner? It was on a par with the Stoke by Nayland arsenic poisonings. He put down a forkful of kipper and let the paper rest on his lap for a moment as he recalled the details of the case.

It must have been four or five years ago. The old man had been found lying face down in a small pond used for watering cattle. There were head injuries but Collins the surgeon had confirmed the cause of death as drowning. The reason for the head injuries was clear: as various witnesses testified, the poor chap had been subjected to regular physical and verbal abuse by his wife and daughter. On the day of his death, they had accused him of being drunk – unjustly, since he had only taken one pint of beer - and the daughter had beaten him about the head with a stick, drawing blood. He had retired to bed but later got up and left the house. He failed to return home that night and his body was discovered by his son the following morning.

The memory of the inquest was still clear in John Wayman's mind. During the proceedings it transpired that Mr Cracknell had on more than one occasion threatened to take his own life, and the jury returned a verdict of suicide by drowning while in a state of temporary mental derangement. However, in view of the unusual circumstances he had felt it appropriate to address the wife and daughter on the barbarity of their conduct and to express his regret that legally they could not be held responsible for a death for which they were morally culpable. Furthermore, he had recommended that the parish officers bring a prosecution at the next January Sessions. He recalled with some satisfaction that his recommendation had been acted upon; the women were duly found guilty of assault and breach of the peace and sentenced to 12 months imprisonment.

But what was this about murder? He picked up the paper and continued reading.

The next few sentences reiterated what he already knew but then came the interesting part:

"On Monday week a private in the Royal African Corps was landed at Portsmouth in confinement, on his own confession of having murdered a man at or near Haverhill four years since, by way-laying him. It appears that the culprit had been liberated from Norwich Castle, a short time previous to his arrival at Haverhill, where he obtained work as a tailor, at Mr Sparshall's of that place; that he was drinking at a public house, and saw the deceased in possession of some money; that he waylaid him, and after he had knocked him down and rifled his pockets, he was alarmed at some noise and threw the body into the ditch, to avoid discovery; that he thence made his way to Long Stratton in Norfolk, where he married; he then, not being able to rest, enlisted, and subsequently committed some offence, to avoid the punishment for which he volunteered into the above regiment, and whilst at Sierra Leone, he made the above confession, and was in consequence sent home by the authorities of that colony."

John Wayman's mind was awash with thoughts. So Martin Cracknell had not committed suicide after all; he had been assaulted for the second time that day by a total stranger, knocked senseless and callously left to drown. May God have mercy on his poor soul. But how had I, the doctor and the jury gotten the verdict wrong? Well, that was understandable: given the knowledge of the first assault, it would have been easy to overlook any evidence of the second. Had those wretched women not beaten the poor man earlier, his injuries might have aroused more suspicion. At least the murderer had been brought to account and would undoubtedly hang. How his conscience must have tormented him these past four years.

"Are you not going to finish your breakfast?" Mrs Wayman looked at the half empty plate, then at her husband and sensed something was troubling him. She laid a hand on his arm. "Was it something you read in the paper?" John sighed. "Remember that poor old boy who was found in the pond in Haverhill…"

The Facts:

Martin Cracknell – sometimes called Cracklin(g) - was my 5th-great grandfather.

He was born about 1752, the son of Martin and Sarah (née Harrington). On 7th November 1775 he married Ann Whiffen at St Mary's Haverhill and they had nine children: William (died in infancy), Ann (died), William (my 4th-great grandfather), Sarah, Martin, Joseph (died), James, Joseph and John. His wife died in June 1799 and just three months later he married Susan Bridge (sometimes known as Susanna) with whom he had a further five children: Ann, Mary, Samuel, Thomas and Elizabeth.

He died on 5th August 1823, his body being found in Reeds Pond*, Haverhill the following morning. The inquest on 7th August returned a verdict of suicide, on the assumption that he had been driven to it by the treatment he received at the hands of his wife and daughter, and the case was reported in some detail in the Cambridge Chronicle of 15th August. He was buried on 8th August.

The possible site of Martin Cracknell's murder

The following January, as reported in the Bury and Norwich Post, Susan and her daughter Mary were convicted of assault and breach of the public peace and sentenced to 12 months in prison. The report noted that "the above prosecution was carried on by the Parish Officers of Haverhill, very much to their credit".

On 24th May 1828 the Norwich Mercury reported the soldier's confession of murder as quoted above.

Susan subsequently married Edward Hymus and died at Great Wratting in 1842.

Mary married David Challis in 1828 and lived to the age of 85. She was buried in Haverhill Cemetery.

Incidentally the family seem to have had several brushes with the law as reported in the local press. In 1814 a magistrate's court had sent Susan to

Bury Gaol "charged with having stolen a pound of butter from the shop of Isaac Wright of Haverhill". In 1806 a Martin Cracknell was sentenced to one month's imprisonment for petty larceny, although it is not clear whether this was the subject of our story or his son.

* I have not been able to establish the location of Reeds Pond, but it seems likely it was somewhere near Reeds Lane, which runs north-east from the town centre towards what would have been fields in the early 19th century. If so, it was possibly filled in when the railway was built in the 1860s. The old postcard reproduced above would seem to imply that that general area was known as Reeds.

Postscript

Looking for information on Mr Wayman the Coroner, I came across a report in The Times in 1827 of an inquest "before Mr John Wayman and a respectable jury" into the deaths of a Mr Simpson and a servant girl at Stoke by Nayland. They had eaten a pudding made by Mrs Simpson, who had unfortunately mistaken a package of arsenic, which her husband had procured for the purpose of destroying rats and left unlabelled in the pantry, for flour. Mr Simpson and the girl died in agony and four others who had eaten rather less of the pudding were rendered seriously ill. A verdict of accidental death was returned.

Mary, John and Mary

It was a Friday evening and the smoke-filled bar of the Black Horse was getting noisy. John Farrant finished his beer, put on his hat and got up to leave. "So which bed is it tonight, John?" someone shouted. If Farrant made a reply it was lost in the ensuing laughter. He stepped out into Camps Road and pulled the door shut behind him.

"Lucky beggar" muttered young Will Beavis. "You think so?" queried Jon Seger, puffing on his pipe. "When you're married, boy, you'll find out one wife is enough." "Or too many" chipped in Bill Claydon and the older men chuckled.

Beavis wasn't contemplating bigamy though; he knew where he'd be going tonight if he were John Farrant. Mary Farrant might have been good looking once, but now she wore her black hair in a tight bun and her thin lips rarely smiled. He compared her mentally with the voluptuous Mary Nunn – and then an unbidden image crossed the young man's mind, that of his mother wagging a finger and scolding "That woman has no shame!". "So what?", he thought, dismissing the unwelcome intrusion, "She has twinkly blue eyes and soft red lips and big…" An elbow in the ribs interrupted his reverie. "Stop daydreaming, young Beavis! It's your round."

Not everyone had laughed when Farrant left the pub. Two men sat in a corner playing dominoes. One of them clenched his fist in silent rage. "What's up, Bor?" asked the other. "Farrant" he growled, half rising to his feet "I could knock his bloody block off!". "Hold you hard, Bor." Bill Sizer put a restraining hand on his friend's arm. "I 'ouldn't pick a fight with him if I was you. He was in Wellington's army. Bayonetted the Frogs like they was tailors' dummies, so I've heard tell." Robert Iron sat down again, seething with anger at the shame the man had brought on his sister.

She meanwhile had just put the children to bed and was sitting at the kitchen table when John Farrant came in through the back door. "Oh, it's you." Her voice was devoid of emotion. "Aren't you pleased to see me?" Receiving no answer, he sat down at the table. "There's bread and cheese in the larder if you're hungry." Mary paused. "Or has *she* fed you?" "I had a bite to eat at the Black Horse."

They sat in silence for a while. It was getting dark, so Mary lit a candle. John looked at his wife and felt the stirring of old feelings. "Mary" he began softly "you remember I always said you looked lovely in the candlelight?" She made no reply. "You still do." He bent forward to kiss her, but she backed away; she wasn't giving in that easily.

~~~~~~~~~~~~

Some Months Later…

Mary happened to be thinking about that evening. She hadn't given in, she'd poured scorn on his flattery and sent him packing, back to his pregnant fancy woman. But one cold January night she'd weakened and let him into her bed – and now, at nearly 40 years old, she was pregnant again too. She already had four children, not counting William who had died aged 11. Enough was enough. She'd find a new home for herself and the children. She had family; her parents were old now, but her brothers, Robert, Daniel and George would help.

~~~~~~~~~~~~

Haverhill, 14 March 1864

Letitia Nunn straightened the bridal veil and told Mary she looked wonderful. How strange it was to be helping her mother prepare to get married - just like her own wedding 14 years ago, but that time it was the normal way round. "Is Mum ready yet?" called her brother John. He looked very smart in his Sunday best suit with a pink carnation in the lapel.

Half an hour later they arrived at the church. As the organist struck up the wedding march, John took his mother's arm and led her down the aisle, while Letitia held the train and her daughter Mary Ann carried the posy. Brother William stood at the chancel steps with their father, his hand suddenly darting to his waistcoat pocket to make sure he still had the ring. It was very much a family affair but there were a few well-wishers in the congregation; no doubt some of them had been here three weeks earlier when John Farrant's first wife was laid to rest.

The Facts:

John Farrant and Mary Nunn were my 3rd-great-grandparents.

John Farrant was born in 1795, the son of John and Ann (née Rooks). He became a soldier, serving with the 51st Light Infantry from 1812-1818, and fought at the Battle of Waterloo. In later life he is variously recorded as being a weaver, labourer and dealer in marine stores.

On 14 September 1812 John married Mary Iron, some six years his senior, at St Mary's, Haverhill. They had had six children between 1813 and 1829: William, Harriet, Emily, William Iron, Hannah and Henry James.

Mary Nunn was born in 1796, the daughter of Thomas and Hannah (née Hunnable). She had ten children between 1820 and 1836, all recorded in the baptismal register of St Mary's as "bb" (base-born). The fifth child, John, has Farrant as his middle name and John Farrant is named as the father of the last five: Letitia, William, twins Mary Ann and Walter, and Joseph. The first four may or may not have been John Farrant's, but the evidence seems to suggest that he was running two households for several years.

The census records indicate that, from 1841 at least, John and Mary (Nunn) were living together in Burton End, Haverhill. In 1851 she was listed as his wife, but this was presumably an assumption on the part of the enumerator. In 1861 she was Mary Nunn, his housekeeper.

Meanwhile his legal wife appears to have reverted to her maiden name. In 1841 she was living in Chauntry Croft, Haverhill, with her children (all using the name Iron) and her widowed father Robert. In 1851 she was listed as Mary Farrant and living with her brother George Iron and his family in Peas Hill Lane. The 1861 census shows Mary Iron, a char woman, living at Crown Passage with her daughter Harriet and grandson William.

John Farrant and Mary Nunn were married on 14th March 1864, his first wife having died a few weeks earlier. Mary died on 18th June 1869. At the time of the 1871 census, John was living as a lodger in the house of Robert Rollinson at Barber's Yard in Steeple Bumpstead. Mary's eldest daughter, now Sarah Tarvin, was living two doors away and was present when John died from gangrene of the foot just five days later.

The Homecoming

Haverhill - 1844

Richard Thake felt a knot in his stomach as the cart trundled through Shudy Camps. Nearly there, he thought. He'd spent the past four days travelling as best he could from Portsmouth and was lucky to have hitched a ride for the last leg of the journey, from Saffron Walden, that morning. "Been away long?" asked the carter. "Oh, it's been a few years." He wasn't going to say fourteen.

The memories of those years ran through his mind again. He and a few mates had stolen sacks of flour from Mr Guy's mill. They were caught and tried at the Bury St Edmunds Summer Sessions on the 19th July 1830, when they were found guilty and sentenced to transportation. The others were given seven years but Thake, with a previous conviction for larceny, got fourteen. After a fortnight in the county gaol they were sent to Portsmouth, where they spent six weeks on the prison hulk *Leviathan* waiting for the next convict ship to sail to Van Diemen's Land.

The *John* left Portsmouth on 9th October with Richard and five of his accomplices among the 200 convicts on board. Those three and a half months at sea were utterly grim. Remarkably no-one died during the voyage – it wasn't uncommon on convict ships.

On 28th January 1831 the *John* docked at Hobart. He recalled the sense of freedom at being released from the cramped, fetid conditions below deck, from which there had only been a few minutes respite two or three times a day. How good the fresh air had smelt as they gazed on the blue hills of their new home. After a few days acclimatisation while aching, wasted muscles were brought back to life, they were assigned to their employers or masters.

Richard was sent to work for a Mr Allenby at Port Arthur. Over the years he tried to keep himself out of mischief, but it was difficult. He recalled the time he spent the night in the barn with Mary Chance the master's servant – three months' hard labour for that one. Then he was caught helping himself to a few eggs – another three months hard labour. As a ploughman back home he'd been used to hard work but breaking stones while wearing chains made every bone in your body ache and was utterly soul-destroying.

But, despite this and a few other lapses – disorderly conduct they called it, it was the thought of Charlotte that kept him going and in 1842 he earned a conditional pardon. Eventually he was granted a passage home.

His thoughts returned to the present as the cart left Nosterfield End and rounded the bend from where the road runs down into Haverhill. Richard craned his neck to see the tower of St Mary's and there it was, just as he remembered it. Gradually more buildings came into view and soon they were rolling along Burton End. He tried not to think of Charlotte. It had been a long time, and anything could have happened…

The cart came to a halt at the top of the High Street. Richard thanked the carter and offered to buy him a beer, but he declined, saying he had business to attend to. Richard walked across to the Rose and Crown, pushed open the door of the public bar and stepped inside.

The chattering fell silent as a dozen or more faces looked at Richard and he looked at them. Edward Jobson was first to break the silence "Good Lord - Richard Thake!" "Ted!" The two men shook hands and exchanged a brief hug. "Well, I be buggered" muttered John Beavis, and a few more acknowledged the home-comer in their laconic Suffolk way. Pints were ordered and no-one noticed the young man in the corner whose face clouded over with an anxious expression; he quickly drained his glass and slipped out.

Stephen Webb was a weaver. That afternoon he was about to finish work and was surprised to see his younger brother at the door. "What's up, Charlie? You look like you've seen a ghost!" "Well, you could say I have. Richard Thake – he's come back!". Then he added "Thought you ought to know. He's in the Rose and Crown." Stephen cursed. Could it be possible? How long had Thake been away? Sure enough, it was fourteen years!

Richard felt that knot in his stomach again as he walked briskly along Downs Lane. The beer had done little to quell his anxiety. Barely an hour ago he hadn't even known if Charlotte was still alive; now he was about to see her again. Would she want him back? Would she even recognise him?

He knocked on the door. After what seemed an eternity but was probably about ten seconds it opened and there stood a lad, tallish and slightly ungainly with the fluffy beginnings of a beard on his chin. Richard could hardly speak. "James?" he croaked, "James Thake?" his voice almost a whisper. James looked perplexed, then slowly he realised the stranger at the door was the father he hadn't seen since he was two. "Dad?!". Richard embraced his son.

It was then he became aware of a younger boy and two small girls hovering in the hallway. The boy reminded him of someone – yes, it was Bill Whiffen. One of the girls ran to the kitchen, calling for her mother.

And then there she was – a little fuller of figure perhaps but still the woman he had loved and married.

Charlotte gasped and stood motionless, her eyes brimming with tears, her brain flooded with conflicting emotions. A moment ago, she hadn't even known whether she would ever see Richard again, now here he was on the doorstep and suddenly she realised she still had feelings towards him. But what would she say to Stephen who had given her emotional and financial support these past few years – and fathered five of her children?

Richard stepped forward hesitantly and Charlotte fell into his arms. There was so much to say but neither of them wanted to speak just yet.

[And there I might have ended the story – except it turns out it wasn't like that at all…]

The Facts:

Richard Thake was my 3rd-great grandfather.

He was born in Haverhill on 30th March 1804, the son of Richard Pament Thake and Elizabeth (née Scotcher), and baptised at St Mary's on 3rd June. On Christmas Eve 1824 he married Charlotte Wright, the daughter of James and Sarah (née Brazier) from Helions Bumpstead. They had two children, Emily who died aged 3 and James (my great-great grandfather).

On 19th July 1830 Richard Thake was convicted of larceny at the Suffolk Quarter Sessions in Bury St Edmunds for his part in a robbery at a flour mill and sentenced to 14 years' transportation (a previous offence being taken into consideration). Six others were convicted of larceny on the same day (though not necessarily in connection with the same incident) and were sentenced to seven years each: John Bigsby, William Townsend, Isaac Potter, Frederick Webb, William Timothy Willis and Thomas Wiffin. All seven were held on the prison hulk *Leviathan* at Portsmouth and all except Wiffin were among 200 convicts sent to Van Diemen's Land (Tasmania) aboard the *John* on 9th October 1830. On arrival Richard was assigned to work for a Mr Allenby in Port Arthur.

Between 1833 and 1844 Charlotte bore another six children, the first fathered by William Whiffen and the others by Stephen Webb. All were known as Thake but given their father's surname as a middle name.

My initial research suggested that Richard served his 14-year sentence and was granted leave to return home. I assumed he was reunited with Charlotte and fathered her last two children, Sarah (born 1846) and Henry (born and died 1848), as no middle name was given to either.

However, fresh information from the Tasmanian Libraries website revealed that he never came back.

His convict record lists a string of misdemeanours: spending the night in a barn with his master's servant Mary Chance (3 months hard labour in chains); pilfering eggs (ditto), disorderly conduct on several occasions, being absent without leave and "visiting an improper house".

Despite these minor offences, he was indeed granted leave to return in 1842. But then he blew it all by stealing a mare, the property of Hugh Germain, and his original 14-year sentence was amended to transportation for life on 21st April 1845. In 1858 he was again in court for stealing £15 from his master, John Derrick, and sentenced to 4 years imprisonment. I have been unable to ascertain the date of his death, but medical records from the same source show he was still alive in Tasmania in 1870.

Stephen Webb was not an uncommon name in the Haverhill area, but it seems most likely that the one who fathered Charlotte's children was born in 1813, the son of Stephen and Elizabeth (née Bradford). He is listed in the 1841 census as living with Charlotte and her children in Downs Lane. He died in 1848, aged 36 and was buried at St Mary's Haverhill on 28th August.

William Whiffen/Whiffing (the name is spelt several different ways in parish records) would appear to have been born in 1810, the son of William and Margaret (née Jones) and younger brother of Thomas, Richard Thake's partner in crime. He died in 1882.

While Thomas Wiffin's conviction was recorded alongside the other six, I can find no record of him actually being transported; indeed, the record of their incarceration on the *Leviathan* shows the other six being sent on the *John* but leaves a blank against him.

The spouse of a transported convict was free to remarry after seven years and Charlotte subsequently married a widower, Charles Rash, in 1855. She must have known him for some time as they were neighbours in 1841 (Downs Lane) and 1851 (Crowland Yard). It is possible that he was the father of Sarah and Henry although his first wife Jane (née Farrant) did not die until 1847. Charles died in 1882. Charlotte died in 1891 and was buried at Haverhill Cemetery on 19th April.

Postscript

Two more interesting details concerning Charlotte's children:

William Whiffen Thake died in 1851 aged 18. The record of his burial on 8th April states "shot himself; acc. death".

Sarah Thake married Ellis Backler in 1869 but appears to have left him soon after. This was probably a wise move on her part, as in 1900 he murdered his common-law wife Louisa Mizen and her twin baby daughters (which he apparently believed were not his) by slitting their throats with a razor. He was sentenced to hang but this was later commuted to life imprisonment on the grounds of insanity. He died in Broadmoor Criminal Asylum in 1919.

Robert and Letitia

"Yu'll be sorry!" Robert Nunn stormed out of the house, slamming the door behind him and leaving Letitia in tears. It was their fourth row in as many days. In 14 years of marriage she'd tried to be a loving and dutiful wife, but he'd become so temperamental lately that she'd begun to wonder whether marrying her cousin had been a ghastly mistake.

Only last year he'd walked out and left her and the children, and they had to rely on charity from the parish and the neighbours. A farm labourer's wages aren't a lot of money but at least it kept a roof over their heads and food on the table. Then when he returned a few weeks later he was arrested and spent six weeks in Bury Gaol. That should have taught him a lesson but for all she knew he'd just abandoned his family for a second time.

But half an hour later Robert came back. He produced a little bottle of reddish-brown liquid from his pocket and held it up in front of her. Letitia felt afraid. "What is it?" she asked, although she probably knew the answer. "Laudanum. Three penn'orth. Should be enough to do the job." And with that he removed the stopper and proceeded to drink the contents.

"Robert! Don't!! Think of the children." But the bottle was already empty.

Letitia was in a state of panic. She had to get help. She rushed into the street, not really knowing where she was going. As luck would have it, she met PC Lott who, on being appraised of the situation, quickly followed her back to the house where Robert was sitting at the kitchen table lolling about and grinning.

Mary Ann and William were looking frightened and confused. They had seen their father drunk before but never in a state like this. PC Lott spoke to them gently and asked them to go to Dr Simpson and tell him there was an urgent case of poisoning.

When Dr Simpson arrived, he looked at Robert, picked up the bottle and smelt it. "Did he drink the whole bottleful?" Letitia nodded tearfully. "He said it was three penn'orth." "Hmmm…" the doctor did a quick mental calculation. "About 60 drops, probably not enough to be fatal." He shook Robert vigorously and made him stand up. Robert staggered and lurched from side to side, still grinning inanely.

"Constable, I want you walk this man round the town until he sobers up. Don't let him out of your sight and if he passes out, bring him back to me as quick as you can." PC Lott groaned inwardly. He was due to finish his beat and go home for tea in less than an hour, but he did as the doctor instructed.

Six hours later Dr Simpson was in his study at *The Mount* when the doorbell rang. Elizabeth answered to find a weary looking policeman and a man who looked a little unsteady on his feet outside. "Sorry to disturb you at this hour Ma'am, but can you tell the doctor Mr Nunn here seems to be recovering." The doctor led Robert into the surgery and bade his wife give the constable a bottle of beer while he examined the patient.

Having taken temperature and pulse and prodded about with his stethoscope and after making him perform a few simple tasks, he pronounced Robert out of danger and sent him home – but not before berating him soundly for the distress he had caused his wife and the trouble to which he had put the unfortunate constable.

The Facts

Robert Nunn was my great-great-grandfather.

He was born on 19th September 1827 at Beggars Row in Haverhill, the sixth child of James (1766-1863) and Sarah (née Farrant, 1791-1840).

On 3rd November 1850 he married his first cousin Letitia Nunn, the illegitimate daughter of Mary Nunn and John Farrant [See *Mary, John and Mary*]. Mary was James' sister. Robert and Letitia were also third cousins on the Farrant side. Neither could read and write, so made their mark on the marriage certificate.

Their first child Mary Ann had already been born on the 7th August that year but died two years later. They had six more children: Sarah (died aged 6), Mary Ann, William Robert (my great-grandfather), Harry, Louisa and George.

In 1861 they were living in Bull Lane, Haverhill, with Mary Ann, William and Harry. Robert's widowed father James was also with them.

On 9th July 1864 Robert was sentenced to six weeks imprisonment in Bury Gaol for the offence of "leaving his family chargeable to Haverhill".

His suicide attempt in 1865 was reported briefly in a local newspaper: "On Wednesday last a man named Robert Nunn attempted to commit suicide by swallowing laudanum. It appears he had some words with his wife, and went out and procured three penny worth of laudanum from Mr. Rose, Chemist, of this town. Returning home, he deliberately drank it off in the presence of his wife. The poor woman was much alarmed, and sent for P.C. Lott, who had the unthankful task of walking the patient about for several hours, until Mr. Simpson, surgeon, pronounced him out of danger."

[Laudanum, a tincture of opium dissolved in alcohol, was a popular remedy during the 19th century and freely available from pharmacies. Overdoses, deliberate or accidental, were not uncommon.]

Robert died of bronchitis and dysentery on 13th February 1866, just a month after the birth of his last child, George, and was buried at St Mary's. George died in May 1867.

In 1871 Letitia was living in Burton End, her profession given as smock maker*. The older children Mary Ann (17), William (14) and Harry (10) were already working, only Louisa (7) was at school.

Letitia subsequently had another daughter Emma (father unknown) who died at the age of 24.

Letitia spent her last days in the Union Workhouse at Kedington, where she died of "senile decay and syncopie" on 22nd September 1901.

According to the 1861 census, William Simpson, General Practitioner, and his wife Elizabeth lived at *The Mount* in Hamlet Road. The best match I can find for PC Lott is Ceilan Lott who in 1871 was listed as a police officer aged 39 at Bury St Edmunds.

* Many Haverhill people were employed in the manufacture of the drabbet smocks worn by farm workers. These were originally woven by hand, but the process was industrialised with the opening of Daniel Gurteen's Chauntry Mills in 1874. There is now a Wetherspoon pub in the town called the Drabbet Smock.

The Sniper's Bullet

Loos, France - October 1915

Reuben groaned as consciousness slowly returned. He'd had that dream again – the one where he was sentenced to death. It always ended the same way - led onto the scaffold, the noose placed around his neck – and then he'd wake up in a cold sweat.

Only this time his face hurt like hell!

Gradually the events of a few hours earlier came back to him. He'd been in the trench, just stood up to stretch his legs and there'd been a whistling sound, a searing pain - and then he'd blacked out. He had a vague recollection of being on a stretcher with the muffled thud of mortar fire in the distance, the stretcher jolting and the bearers swearing as their boots slipped on the muddy ground.

But here he was lying in a bed. He couldn't see much and raised a hand to find his head was swathed in bandages. He might have drifted off again, but a voice with a reassuringly familiar Suffolk accent was calling his name "Hello Reuben, how you feelin'?"

He opened his eyes to find the MO leaning over him. "You're a lucky ol' bugger, Bor. Thet bullet had your number on it for sure. Another inch and you'd ha' been a goner. Made a right ol' mess of your cheek, though."

Reuben tried to speak but the pain and the effort were too much. The MO nodded, "I'll give you another shot of morphine. Best thing you can do for now is sleep."

As the morphine took effect and the pain began to subside, Reuben thought about Rose and baby Stanley. He'd hardly seen his son. He and Rose had been planning to marry last year but then the war got in the way; he joined Kitchener's New Army (7th Battalion, Suffolk Regiment) at Bury St Edmunds and started training and the wedding had to wait a few weeks – and in the meantime Stanley came along. Still, putting the cart before the horse was nothing unusual in Haverhill.

He thought of his mother, Emma – just as well she doesn't know I've been shot; she must be worried sick about us anyway. He wondered how his brothers were doing. Were they all still alive even? Percy and Albert were the professionals, having joined the Suffolk Regiment before the war. Frank signed up for the 8th Battalion in July. They'd always been close, he and Frank, and Frank was courting Rose's little sister Nellie. David joined the 12th Battalion around the same time. Ezra had managed to avoid being called up. Perhaps I should have been a shopkeeper too thought Reuben ruefully.

His mind drifted back to childhood at Lilley Cottage in Withersfield. It was a bit crowded and noisy with 15 children growing up – could have been worse if Percy and Albert hadn't joined the army and Alma gone into service before the younger ones came along. It was always quiet on Sundays though; their father had forbidden them to speak on the Lord's Day, so they devised their own sign language until he realised what was going on and forbade that too in case they were talking about him behind his back.

Reuben began dozing off. There was a hymn tune running though his head "Lead kindly light amid the encircling gloom, lead Thou me on", along with images of St Mary's church where he and his siblings used to sing in the choir. And there were mushrooms, big ones, that grew among the tombstones. Then he was seeing the sun set over the yew trees and the tower. And in the encircling gloom he fell asleep.

William and Emma Nunn with (L-R) Christopher, Reuben, David, Frank, Percy and Albert.

The Facts

Reuben Charles Nunn (1891-1961) was my paternal grandfather.

He was the fourth of 15 children born to William and Emma (née Medcalf) between 1886 and 1911 in Withersfield, Suffolk. In January 1915 he married Rose Lily Thake, their son Stanley having been born a few weeks earlier. His younger brother Frank later married her sister Ellen (Nellie).

Six of the brothers* served in the First World War: Percy, Albert, Reuben, Frank, David, and later Christopher (he would have been too young at the beginning). All six lived to tell the tale, although Reuben nearly didn't; he was shot in the cheek by a German sniper. I'm not certain it was at the Battle of Loos, but that seems the most likely possibility; it was one of the major campaigns in which the 7th Battalion fought and there were heavy casualties, particularly among the inadequately trained new recruits.

And yes, Reuben did have that recurring dream, although possibly not at that stage of his life.

And mushrooms still grow in Withersfield churchyard.

* Ezra, the third eldest, appears to have been exempt from military service.

The Last Banana

Haverhill - 13th January 1926

"Can I have a banana please, Daddy?"

Rueben fetched the last banana from the fruit bowl. Bananas were a luxury and they probably wouldn't be getting any more anytime soon, but the lad was poorly, and it might do him some good or at least cheer him up. He partly peeled the banana and handed it to young Bill who was sitting propped up in bed. The boy took it and began to eat it slowly. After the last mouthful he laid down as if to sleep and Reuben tucked the bedclothes around him.

About an hour later Reuben was in the shed. He could hear his daughter May singing and was thinking what a sweet voice she has. Suddenly Rose was shouting frantically from the back door: "Reuben, come here!". He rushed into the house. There was sheer panic in his wife's eyes. "He's stopped breathing" she gasped.

Reuben shouted to his older son "Stan, go and fetch the doctor – quick as you can." He went into the bedroom and bent over the small figure lying there. Sure enough, there was no sign of breathing. He took the boy's wrist. The little hand was limp and cool and there was no discernible pulse.

He became aware of May standing in the doorway. She had stopped singing and burst into tears. Reuben put his arm tenderly round her shoulder, not knowing what to say. Five-year-old Jack looked confused, but in his young mind he knew that something bad was happening.

20 minutes later the doctor arrived. He took out his stethoscope and briefly examined his young patient before shaking his head. "I'm so sorry, Mr and Mrs Nunn. There's nothing I can do."

Then Stan came back, having thoughtfully been down the road to fetch Aunt Nellie, who took one look at the scene, then threw her arms around her sister and the two of them wept uncontrollably.

The Facts

William George Nunn was the uncle I never knew. He died of bronchial pneumonia on the 13th of January 1926 aged six. Jack recalled that Bill asked his father for a banana shortly before he died.

Hokey Pokey

Hokey pokey, penny a lump, that's the stuff to make you jump.

Haverhill – 1930s

Jack finished his paper round and cycled up the frying pan alley that was Helions Park Grove. Leaning his bike against the side of the house, he went in the back door and sat at the kitchen table. His mother turned the gas cooker on, put a fresh knob of lard in the still warm frying pan and began cooking. She ladled bacon, eggs and fried bread onto a plate and put it in front of him. "You're lucky to get any eggs this morning, they nearly went in there." She nodded towards the big pan at the other end of the table, in which a creamy mixture of eggs, milk, sugar and vanilla essence was slowly cooling.

Rose gave the contents of the pan a half-hearted stir and then looked hard at her son. "Time you got a proper job" she said, "I've asked at Gurteen's and they might be able to take you on." Jack grimaced. The thought of working in that factory didn't appeal one bit - even if it might mean he could afford a decent racing bike with gears. He ate the greasy food in silence. "Your father could do with some help. He's in the shed."

That last piece of information was entirely superfluous. The sound of hymn tunes played on an accordion had been wafting into the kitchen during Jack's breakfast. Besides, Dad was always in the shed every morning.

The custard should have cooled down by now. Reuben put down the accordion, placed the ice cream tub in front of him and began unwrapping the blocks of ice which had been delivered that morning wrapped in sacking. "Ah, Jack, give me a hand will you." He handed the lad a hammer and chisel and Jack broke up the ice while Reuben packed it into the outer tub, adding a handful of coarse salt now and then. He fetched the big pan of custard from the kitchen and poured it carefully into the inner tub while Jack stood by with the wooden paddle. Then he took the remaining ice and filled the icebox on the trike.

~~~~~~~~~~

It was a warm summer's afternoon. The school doors opened, and a horde of children poured out towards the gate. A few drifted up Withersfield Road or towards the station, but the majority went up Queen Street and turned into Camps Road, heading for the Recreation Ground. Freda Nunn stood on the corner, clutching the penny in her pocket, while she waited for her big sister Joyce. Then the two of them joined the straggling procession.

The clanging of a handbell greeted them as they approached the Rec. "I bet it's the Walls man" scowled Joyce. It was. He'd positioned his trike on the corner of Camps Road and Chauntry Road, so the children had to walk past him. Freda didn't like the Walls man; he had an ugly red nose and a smarmy grin - even his bell sounded horrid. Fortunately, a couple of new kids had succumbed to his call and he was busy serving them, so the sisters quickly dived past him and went along the edge of the Rec towards Mill Hill. A few others were already waiting there.

Freda, lying on the grass, was beginning to feel bored and was contemplating making a daisy chain, while Joyce was wondering what strategy they should adopt if the Walls man had run out of customers and decided to come round to their corner, when they heard another bell and a cheery call of "Hokey Pokey!" – and there was Uncle Reuben, pedalling along in his white coat and flat cap. The trike rolled to a halt, Reuben applied the brake and the little crowd of children surged round him.

Freda put her hand in her pocket. It was empty! "I've lost my penny" she wailed. "When did you last have it?" asked Joyce. "I don't know. I had it when we came out of school." "Well, that's not much help." Needle in a haystack thought Joyce, who didn't fancy retracing their steps looking for a penny that some other kid had probably picked up by now anyway.

"What's the matter, Freda?" Reuben, who had finished serving the others, looked at the tearful little face. "She's lost her penny, Uncle Reuben." "Well, never you mind. Have this one on me, both of you" he said softly and filled two cones.

The two girls thanked him profusely and walked slowly across the Rec, licking their ice creams. The Walls man gave them a dirty look as he pedalled off down Burton End. Freda stuck her tongue out behind his back.

The Facts

During the 1930s Reuben Nunn ran a small business making ice cream in his shed at 5 Helions Park Grove, Haverhill, and selling it from a "stop me and buy one" tricycle. Family members who were children at the time recalled that they used to avoid the Wall's ice cream man and wait for Uncle Reuben with his superior home-made product.

Joyce and Freda were the daughters of Reuben's brother Albert.

The Fifteen

William and Emma Nunn had fifteen children between 1886 and 1911. All survived to adulthood and lived their "three score years and ten", which is all the more remarkable considering that six of the boys served in the army during the First World War.

William and Emma Nunn with 10 of their 15 children (c.1910)
Back row (L-R): Reuben & Frank
Middle row: David, Stella (baby), Christopher, Ruth & Louis
Front row: Frederick, Laura & Violet Grace

Percy William Nunn (1886-1967)
Married (1915) Melinda May Siggs.

Albert Arthur Nunn (1888-1988)
Married (1924) Ethel Maud Tilbrook.

Ezra James Nunn (1889-1967)
Married (1912) Mary Jane Moore.

Reuben Charles Nunn (1891-1961)
Married (1915) Rose Lily Thake.

Alma Emma Nunn (1893-1987)
Married (1920) Bertie Harry Chalk; (1923) Joseph Samuel Read.

Frank Nunn (1895-1978)
Married (1919) Ellen (Nellie) Thake, sister of Rose.

David Joe Nunn (1896-1969)
Married (1924) Emily Hazel Thelma Brakewell; (1934) Ivy Gwendoline Wood.

Ruth Amelia Nunn (1898-1991)
Married (1926) William John Kiddy.

Christopher Nunn (1899-1983)
Married (1926) Undine Simes; (1947) May Hedges.

Louis Edward Nunn (1901-1986)
Married (1924) Florence Lillian Basham

Laura Nunn (1904-1977)
Married (1925) Robert Jack Parker.

Violet Grace Nunn (1905-1993)
Married (1930) Sydney Joseph Smith.

Frederick Norman Nunn (1907-1989)
Married (1932) Eileen Turner.

Stella May Nunn (1909-2002)
Married (1944) John Garnett.

Bryce Phillip Nunn (1911-1995)
Married (1937) Doris Annie Edith Pettitt.

Percy worked as a road sweeper, always wore wellington boots and had a reputation as "the best swearer in Haverhill" (though, as one of my cousins observed, he'd have a bit more competition nowadays).

Albert lived to receive his telegram from the Queen and sang "The Old Rugged Cross" at his 100th birthday party.

Ezra took a job in the village shop and subsequently married his widowed employer, Mary Ann Moore. He kept the shop, which stood on the edge of Withersfield village green, until his death in 1967. It's not there now but the place is still known locally as Nunn's Corner.

Alma emigrated to the USA in 1922, her first marriage having not lasted long. She subsequently remarried and lived the rest of her life in

Pennsylvania.

David and Christopher emigrated to New Zealand in 1920. They had one suitcase between them, which burst open and scattered their clothes on the quay as they were about to board the ship. Christopher apparently walked off and left David to deal with it.

Ruth lived in Withersfield all her life. She was an accomplished crochet worker and made gifts for the Queen and Prince and Princess of Wales for which she received letters of thanks from Buckingham Palace.

Bryce lived in Norwich and was involved in the initial trial of postcodes in 1959.

The Nunn / Farrant Line

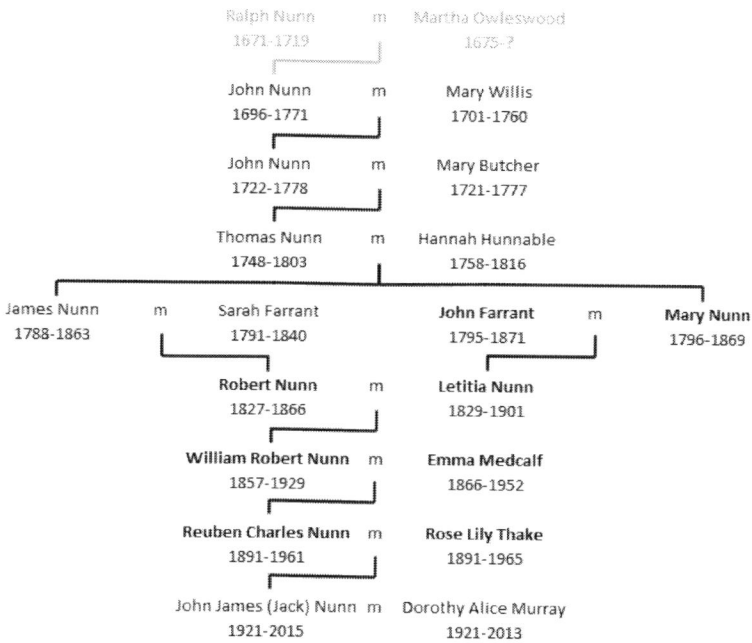

Ralph Nunn   m   Martha Owleswood
1671-1719   1675-?

John Nunn   m   Mary Willis
1696-1771   1701-1760

John Nunn   m   Mary Butcher
1722-1778   1721-1777

Thomas Nunn   m   Hannah Hunnable
1748-1803   1758-1816

James Nunn   m   Sarah Farrant   John Farrant   m   Mary Nunn
1788-1863   1791-1840   1795-1871   1796-1869

Robert Nunn   m   Letitia Nunn
1827-1866   1829-1901

William Robert Nunn   m   Emma Medcalf
1857-1929   1866-1952

Reuben Charles Nunn   m   Rose Lily Thake
1891-1961   1891-1965

John James (Jack) Nunn   m   Dorothy Alice Murray
1921-2015   1921-2013

The Medcalf / Cracknell Line

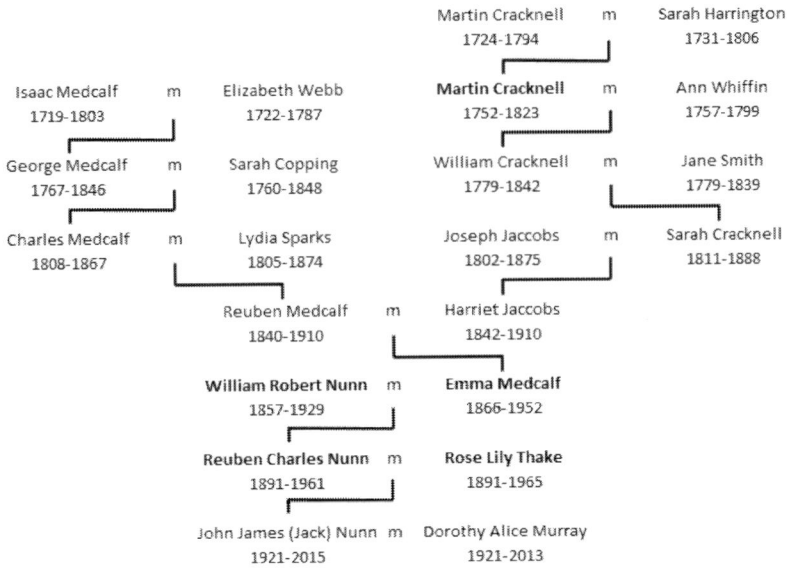

Martin Cracknell   m   Sarah Harrington
1724-1794   1731-1806

Isaac Medcalf   m   Elizabeth Webb   **Martin Cracknell**   m   Ann Whiffin
1719-1803   1722-1787   1752-1823   1757-1799

George Medcalf   m   Sarah Copping   William Cracknell   m   Jane Smith
1767-1846   1760-1848   1779-1842   1779-1839

Charles Medcalf   m   Lydia Sparks   Joseph Jaccobs   m   Sarah Cracknell
1808-1867   1805-1874   1802-1875   1811-1888

Reuben Medcalf   m   Harriet Jaccobs
1840-1910   1842-1910

William Robert Nunn   m   **Emma Medcalf**
1857-1929   1866-1952

Reuben Charles Nunn   m   **Rose Lily Thake**
1891-1961   1891-1965

John James (Jack) Nunn   m   Dorothy Alice Murray
1921-2015   1921-2013

The Thake Line

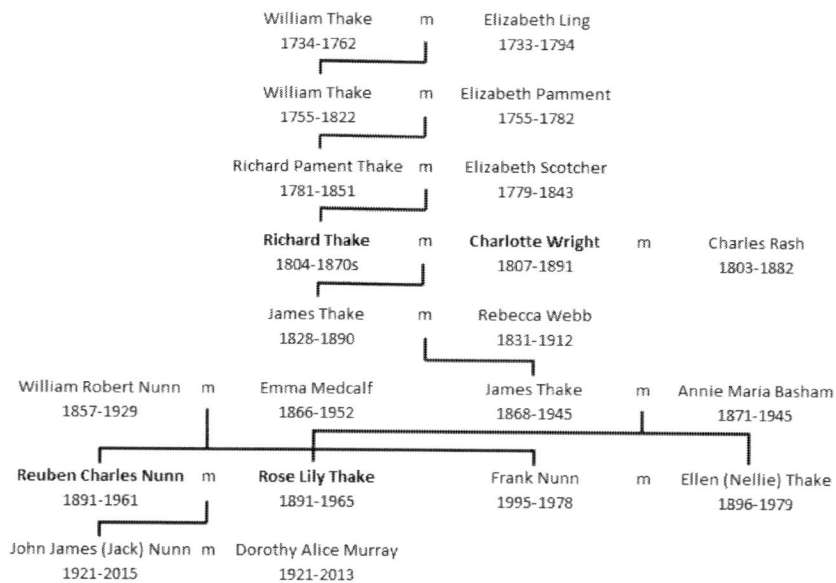

William Thake   m   Elizabeth Ling
1734-1762   1733-1794

William Thake   m   Elizabeth Pamment
1755-1822   1755-1782

Richard Pament Thake   m   Elizabeth Scotcher
1781-1851   1779-1843

Richard Thake   m   **Charlotte Wright**   m   Charles Rash
1804-1870s   1807-1891   1803-1882

James Thake   m   Rebecca Webb
1828-1890   1831-1912

William Robert Nunn   m   Emma Medcalf   James Thake   m   Annie Maria Basham
1857-1929   1866-1952   1868-1945   1871-1945

Reuben Charles Nunn   m   **Rose Lily Thake**   Frank Nunn   m   Ellen (Nellie) Thake
1891-1961   1891-1965   1995-1978   1896-1979

John James (Jack) Nunn   m   Dorothy Alice Murray
1921-2015   1921-2013

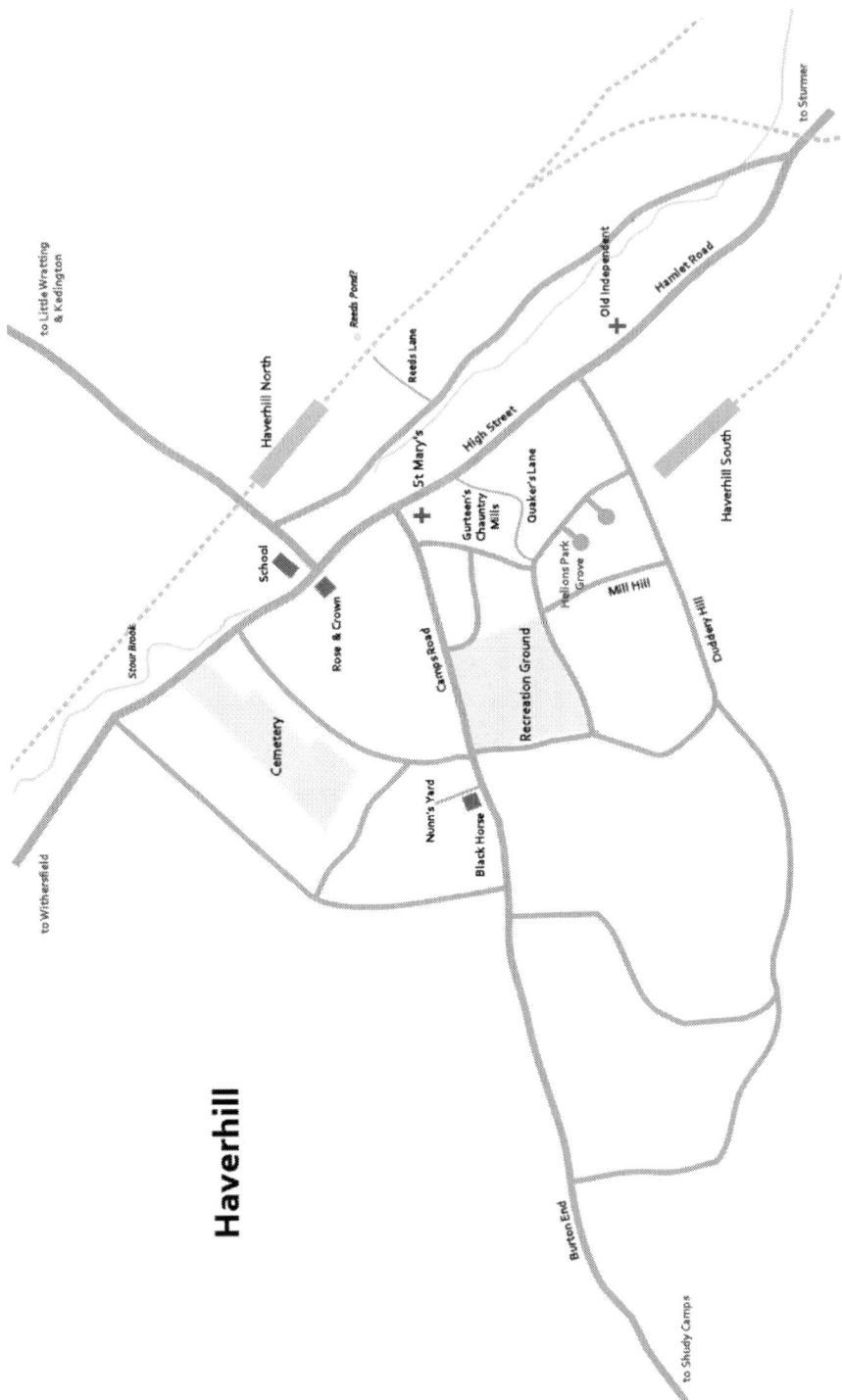

Haverhill

to Little Wratting
& Kedington

Haverhill North

Reeds Pond?

Reeds Lane

St Mary's

High Street

Quaker's Lane

Gurteen's
Chauntry
Mills

Old Independent

Hamlet Road

to Sturmer

Haverhill South

Mill Hill

Hellions Park
Grove

Dudery Hill

School

Rose & Crown

Stour Brook

Cemetery

Camps Road

Recreation Ground

Nunn's Yard

Black Horse

to Witchersfield

Burton End

to Study Camps

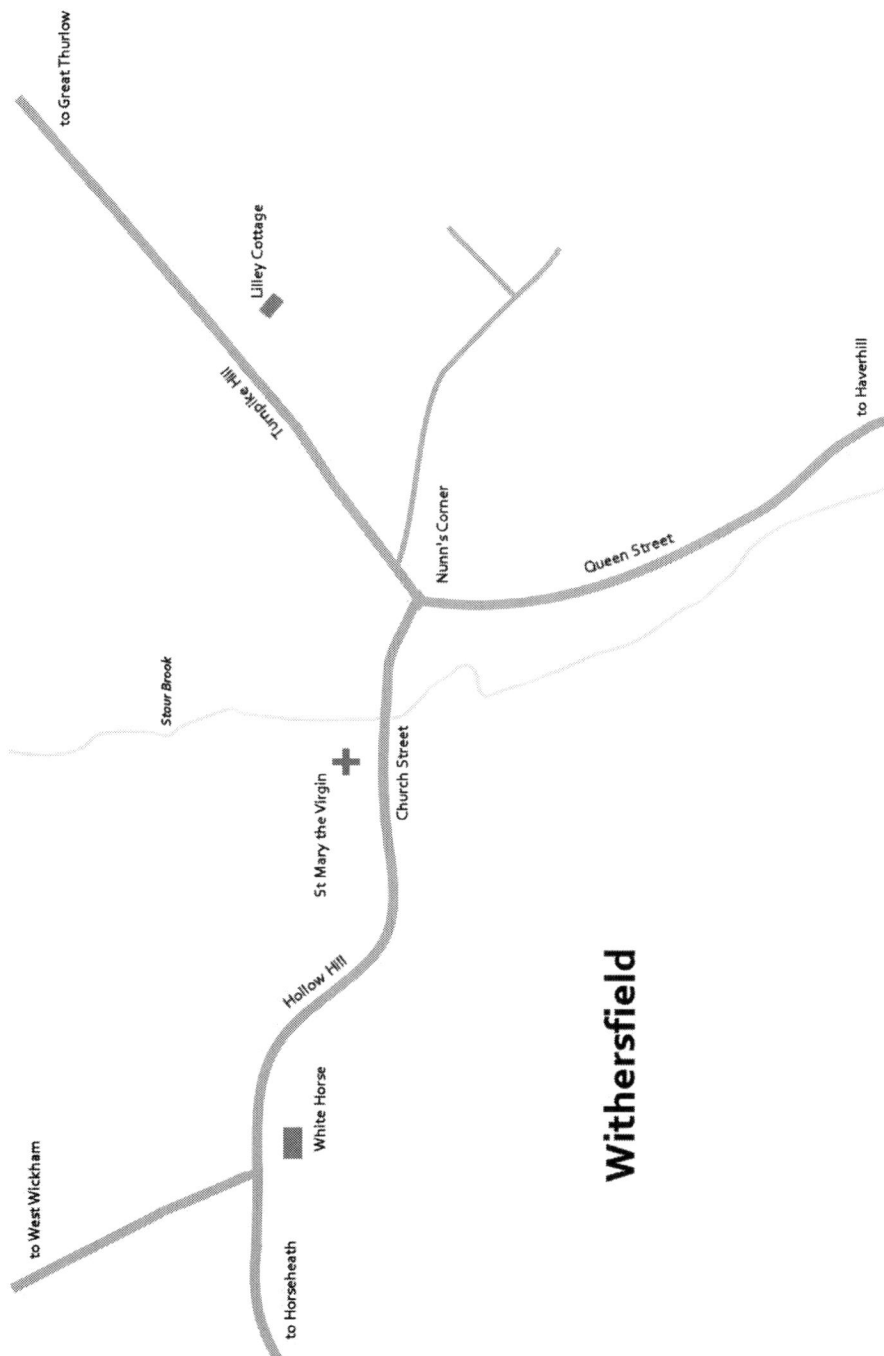

Withersfield

to Great Thurlow

Lilley Cottage

Turnpike Hill

Nunn's Corner

Queen Street

to Haverhill

Stour Brook

St Mary the Virgin

Church Street

Hollow Hill

White Horse

to West Wickham

to Horseheath

Jack Nunn with his cycling trophies (c. 1948)

Reuben Nunn and an accordion similar to his

Reuben and Rose Nunn with Stanley and May (c. 1919)

Emma Nunn (née Medcalf)

St Mary the Virgin, Withersfield

Reuben and Harriet Medcalf

Ezra's shop at Nunn's Corner, Withersfield, from the church tower

The Union Workhouse at Kedington

The Murray Side

They that go down to the sea in ships

Tabitha

"Eli, I baptise thee in the name of the Father" – splosh – "and of the Son" – splosh, whimper – "and of the Holy Ghost" – splosh, "Waaaaah!".

One of the wardens handed the minister a linen cloth with which he wiped the baby's face before continuing "We receive this child into the Congregation of Christ's flock, and do sign him with the sign of the Cross, in token that hereafter he shall not be ashamed to confess the faith of Christ crucified, and manfully to fight under His banner against sin, the world, and the devil, and to continue Christ's faithful soldier and servant unto his life's end." He quickly returned the baby to his mother's arms as the congregation replied "Amen". Tabitha clutched the child to her bosom, rocking him gently, and within seconds he was fast asleep.

At the end of the service George Lampshire shook the minister's hand warmly and thanked him. He then looked around for his wife. She was still sitting in the pew with the baby on her lap and her head bowed as if she were deep in thought or some private reverie.

And indeed she was. Tabitha's mind had gone back to the christening of her first child 25 years earlier. It wasn't a joyous occasion like today with the little village church filled with family and neighbours. As a girl of 17 with her tiny baby she had felt anxious - frightened even – and the big church of Ss Peter and Paul Fareham seemed empty and cold. She recalled the priest's voice echoing round the building and her own voice barely audible as her dry mouth responded to "Name this child" with "Jane".

Tabitha was born in Bermondsey in south London but after her parents died, she was sent to live with relatives in Fareham. At 16 she met Thomas Powell from Titchfield who worked in one of the local shipyards. She blushed at the thought of that day in the Great Beeche Wood when they became more than friends. It was there too that she confided to him a few weeks later that she was carrying his child. He told her not to worry; they would get married soon and have many children.

Then Tabitha's world fell apart. There was an accident at the shipyard when some scaffolding collapsed, and Thomas's ribs were crushed by a large baulk of timber. He died two days later. Even now tears would come to her eyes as she recalled him lying in bed, holding her hand and telling her between gasps of pain that they'd get married as soon as he was better, although both of them knew it wasn't going to happen.

When Jane was christened, Tabitha already knew she wouldn't be able to keep her. It was in the child's best interest they told her. Mr Gear the Parish Clerk at Alverstoke and his wife had offered to adopt Jane. Tabitha felt helpless with no-one she could turn to. For the next year and a half it seemed that life was nothing but misery and despair, until a kindly woman befriended her and invited her to the local chapel. And then she met George.

George Lampshire was a Cornish miner but occasionally entrusted by the mine owners with accompanying shipments of valuable metals – which might otherwise provide easy pickings for unscrupulous dockers - from Falmouth to other ports on the south coast. George, being a trustworthy young man from a God-fearing non-conformist family, was a natural choice for the job. And so it was that he happened to be at the chapel in Fareham one Sunday morning and was immediately taken with the pretty but unhappy girl in the next pew.

On his next visit to Fareham, he proposed to her. They were married at the chapel a few weeks later and Tabitha set out to begin a new life in Cornwall.

But for the moment she couldn't help thinking about Jane. She would be 26 now. Was she still in Alverstoke? Was she married with children of her own?

"Are you all right, Mama?" Her daughter Sarah was tugging at her sleeve. "Yes dear, I was just thinking." Tabitha let go of her thoughts and smiled. "We must go and cut the christening cake."

The Facts

Tabitha Thorne was my 4th-great-grandmother.

My 3rd-great-grandmother Jane Powell was baptised at Ss Peter and Paul, Fareham on 5th December 1799. Her mother's name is given as Tabitha Thorne. There is no record of the father, but his name was presumably Powell.

On 7th December 1802 Tabitha Thorne married George Lampshire at Fareham.

Eli Lampshier was born on 20th December 1825 and baptised at St Allen near Truro on 26th February 1826. The ceremony took place in the parish church but was conducted by a minister of the Truro Bible Christian Circuit. The record is unusually detailed and states that Eli was "the son of

George Lampshier of the Parish of St Allen County of Cornwall, Miner, and Tabitha his wife (who was the daughter of Peter and Mary Thorne)".

In 1841 George and Tabitha Lampshire, both aged 50, were living in Perranzabuloe with daughter Sarah 25 and son Eli 15. There are 'Y's in the "Born in same county" column (but I can find no record of Tabitha Thorne being born in Cornwall around the right time).

A Tabitha Thorn was born on 31st December 1779 to Peter and Mary Thorn and baptised on 8th February 1780 at St Mary Magdalene, Bermondsey, then in the county of Surrey.

And a little speculation…

The Bermondsey dates could be consistent with the birth of Jane and marriage to George Lampshire. However, 1779 seems a little early to be consistent with Eli's birth and the ages in 1841 which – even allowing for the fact that in the 1841 census adults' ages were commonly rounded down to the nearest 5 years - suggest Tabitha was born no earlier than 1785. If it were not for the comparatively unusual names involved, I would have rejected the notion that all the events refer to the same person, but for the moment I'm treating it as a possibility (and allowing a little flexibility in the dates).

What became of Mr Powell? Was he the sort of cad who would simply abandon a pregnant teenager to her fate? A sailor on shore leave in Portsmouth perhaps? But, as Jane was given his name, I chose to assume for the purposes of my story that he died tragically before he could make an honest woman of Tabitha. Maybe he was the Thomas Powell who was buried at Titchfield on the 11th October 1799, but I doubt we shall ever know.

One thing we do know is that when Jane Powell married John Murray at Alverstoke in 1819 it was with the consent (she was still a minor) of Joseph Gear the Parish Clerk, so it seems reasonable to assume that he was her adopted father or legal guardian.

Pilot Murray

The town of Lymington in Hampshire stands at the mouth of the eponymous river (the confluence of several small streams rising in the New Forest) which flows into the Solent through a broad estuary, forming a natural harbour. Formerly a busy port, it is now chiefly a centre for yachting (stand on the Quay and look seawards and the river is a veritable forest of masts) and a terminus for the Isle of Wight ferries.

Lymington High Street with Pilot Murray on the right

Lymington – 1860s

William Dempster Murray was a Trinity Pilot. It was an important job. There are treacherous currents in the Solent where it narrows to less than a mile between Hurst Spit and Fort Albert and his task was to guide ships safely though that narrow strait and in and out of Lymington harbour. His portly figure was a familiar sight around the town.

One morning as he walked up Quay Hill, he noticed a small crowd gathered round an artist seated at an easel. He stopped to look. The man was making sketches of the High Street. "This is Mr Murray, the Pilot" said someone, and before long, notwithstanding the fact that he had been looking forward to his lunch, he had been persuaded to stand outside the shop at the bottom of the High Street, looking suitably important…

The Facts

William Dempster Murray was my great-great-grandfather.

He was born in 1821 at Bembridge on the Isle of Wight. Later the family moved to Lymington when his father, John Murray, retired from the sea and became the landlord of the Ship Inn on the Quay.

In 1841 William Dempster was a lodger in the home of Anthony and Frances Ibbitson at Bishop Wearmouth, County Durham, when his occupation is given as mariner. On 16th March the following year he married the Ibbitsons' daughter Jane at Monk Wearmouth and brought her back to Lymington.

The next three censuses show them living at Waterloo Place or Quay Street, Lymington and his occupation is given as (Trinity) Pilot.

The engraving which resulted from the artist's sketches has been widely copied. At one time it was used as a placemat in the dining room of the Stanwell House Hotel. A copy hangs over my desk as I write.

Granny Griggs's Pig

The village of Brockenhurst is in the New Forest about four miles inland from Lymington. The Weir, a tributary of the Lymington River, flows through the village, crossing the main street in a shallow (for most of the year) ford known as the Watersplash.

Brockenhurst, 1850s

Jane paid the baker and put the two loaves of bread in her basket which she then placed on the floor. Piggy grunted, thrust his snout forward and grasped the handle in his teeth. "Good afternoon, Mrs Griggs". It was Miss Ash the schoolmistress. "How is your cow today?" "A little better, thank you, Miss Ash" replied Jane and then struck up a conversation about her daughter's schooling.

Five minutes later, two little boys stuck their heads round the baker's door. "Mrs Griggs, Mrs Griggs, we just seen Piggy going down the road!" Sure enough, the pig had gone – with the basket. Jane groaned. It wasn't that she'd lose him; he could find his own way home, but he might bump into something and upset the basket. Or he might go through the Watersplash. He *would* go through the Watersplash, he always did. It wouldn't be the first time she arrived home with a basket of soggy bread. She made her excuses to Miss Ash, who nodded sympathetically, and hurried out of the shop.

Several people in the High Street had seen the pig, trotting along with the basket as he had done twice a week for the past two or three years. Nearing the Watersplash, she still hadn't caught up with him. It wouldn't matter so much in the summer when the stream was a mere trickle, but at this time of year the water was quite high. And there he was, in the middle of the road, not wading but rolling a foot deep in water. "Piggy!!" she yelled.

"Don't worry, dear." It was Mrs Jenvey, standing by the footbridge holding the basket. "I managed to rescue your shopping." "Oh, thank you! I thought for a moment it was on its way down to Lymington." Mrs Jenvey laughed. "Looks as if he's enjoying himself." The two women chatted for a while as Piggy continued his bath and then rolled in the grass. Jane crossed the bridge and gave the basket back to the pig who followed her obediently up Rhinefield Road.

~~~~~~~~~~~~~~~

John Griggs finished his breakfast. "The butcher's coming today." "Why, John?" Jane paused. "Not Piggy! Oh, how could you?" "Don't be so sentimental, woman" said John, pulling his boots on "Pigs are for eating." "But he's like part of the family. We raised him from a piglet and looked after him like a child." "So? Your father treated his sheep like children, but he always knew they'd end up on someone's dinner table." And with that he went out to mend the leak in the barn.

Jane couldn't concentrate on her baking. She was still trying to stifle her tears when the butcher arrived. "John says you've got a pig for slaughtering." He looked round the yard. "Not that one that carries your basket, is it?" he asked and then felt awkward as the answer was written all over her face. "You'd best speak to John" she said and went back indoors.

Shortly afterwards Elizabeth came home from school. "Mummy, why is the butcher here?" She looked at her mother's face – and burst into tears.

Ten minutes later John stormed into the kitchen, followed by the butcher. "Where *is* that pig? We can't find him anywhere." He looked half-accusingly at his wife. "I don't know. I haven't seen him since I milked the cows this morning." "Well, we've searched the barn and the outhouse and the milking shed. He's not in the field or down by the pond." "No, I haven't hidden him, if that's what you're thinking, so it's no good looking at me like that. I don't know where he is." The butcher looked uncomfortable. "It's OK, John, I'll come another day." He left quickly.

Supper at Ober Farm was eaten in silence that evening. Elizabeth went upstairs to finish her homework. And there was Piggy, asleep in her bed. She thought of smuggling him out of the house, but her involuntary scream of surprise had already alerted her parents.

Jane looked at her husband. "I told you he was part of the family." "I guess he is" said John softly, putting an arm round his wife and daughter. "I'll tell the butcher we're keeping him."

So Piggy lived to shop another day.

The Facts

Jane Curtis (1820-1869) was my great-great-grandmother.

She was the daughter of Thomas Curtis, a shepherd, and Martha (née Hampton) aka Patty, who lived at Sandy Down in the parish of Brockenhurst.

On 8th November 1839 she married John Griggs (1803-1864) at Boldre church.

John Griggs was born in Boldre and it appears that his mother Catherine died soon after giving birth. I have been unable to find any baptismal records for Catherine or her husband, John Griggs senior, so it may be that they were not native to the area [See *A Long Shot*].

In 1841 and 1851 John and Jane were living at Palmer's Water in Brockenhurst and his occupation is recorded as agricultural labourer, but by 1861 they had moved to Ober Farm in Rhinefield Road. I assume it was either a smallholding or they were tenant farmers (most farms in the area were owned by the Morant family of Brockenhurst Park). Miss Ash was the village schoolmistress at this time.

My grandmother Alice Mary House (Jane's granddaughter) used to tell the story of Granny Griggs's Pig, who carried her shopping basket in his mouth, couldn't be found when the butcher came round and was later found asleep in a bed. If he had a name other than Piggy, I don't think I was ever told it.

Incidentally, there is a Grigg Lane in Brockenhurst. Whether it has any connection with my ancestors I have no idea.

Is the Back Door Open?

Lymington - 1896

Elizabeth Andrews finished clearing away the family's supper and had a few brief words with her husband James who nodded sympathetically as she slipped out of the house. She turned right out of Spring Road into Queen Katherine Road and walked briskly; in five minutes she was back at her mother's house for the third time that day.

She met the doctor in the hallway. "Ah, Mrs Andrews… It's only a matter of time, I'm afraid." His demeanour and the tone of his voice made the words almost superfluous. "I've given her a mild sedative. She should be quite comfortable but do call me if she's in any distress." Elizabeth thanked him and went upstairs. She was glad she had called the Vicar that morning and he'd been able to give her mother communion.

Jane was drifting in and out of consciousness as scenes from her life floated around her head like pictures in a gallery. She remembered her childhood in Sunderland, playing by the River Wear with her sister Frances, going to her father's workplace and watching the glassblowers at work.

When she was a little older, the Ibbitsons had a spare bedroom in their house on Ayer's Quay and used to take in short-term lodgers, mostly seamen from the nearby Sunderland Docks. Some of them could be quite unpleasant, particularly when they'd just come off a ship, spent half their wages in the pub and Jane and Frances were the first girls they'd seen for weeks. But William Murray was different – a year older than her, he was handsome and well-spoken. Jane took an instant liking to him - and he to her. The next time he was in Sunderland they met again.

They were married the following spring in the old church of St Peter's in Monkwearmouth. Then Jane faced the biggest upheaval of her life – leaving her family and friends and sailing south with her new husband.

She recalled leaving Portsmouth on the last leg of the journey and William pointing out landmarks as they sailed down the Solent. There ahead were the Needles on the left and Hurst Castle on the right but the ship was already turning into the channel between the mudflats that line the mouth of the Lymington River. "There's Jack in the Basket" said William "Nearly there!". Then he was waving towards the Ship Inn on the Quay where his father was landlord. Jane immediately warmed to her father-in-law. Like her, he was from the north-east but after years of shipping coal from

Tyneside he had settled in Lymington and become a publican.

William was then studying to be a Trinity House Pilot. She was so proud of him when he obtained his certificate and took on the important job of guiding ships from the English Channel through the narrow strait between Hurst Spit and Fort Albert, where the currents could be so treacherous if you didn't know the tides, and in and out of Lymington Harbour. And of course it meant he wasn't away for weeks on end like most mariners were.

As the years went by William's stature increased – in more ways than one. She'd often remarked that as the esteem in which he was held by the townsfolk increased so did the size of his belly. Jane thought of the engraving which hung in the drawing room downstairs - she could picture it in her mind's eye with William's portly figure in his black suit and top hat standing outside the shop at the bottom of the High Street. Dear William, he'd always provided for her every need and, although he'd been gone eight years now, she could still consider herself a woman of independent means.

Jane became aware of her eldest daughter sitting by the bedside knitting. Elizabeth noticed she was awake and wiped her brow. "Are you comfortable?". "Yes, dear." Jane closed her eyes again. Elizabeth had been so good and loyal to her, as had her husband. James came from Yarmouth, just a few miles across the Solent. His father had been a pilot and now he was one too. Perhaps he'd be on an engraving of the High Street one day.

Jane thought of her other children. She and William had had five girls and five boys and they all survived to adulthood apart from little Sophia. Sadly David had died two years ago.

Anthony was a fine sailor, skipper of an ocean-going yacht. And his son, young Tom, kept the family tradition going. Since he was 13 he'd been off to Africa for two or three months at a time – but he always came to see her when he was home.

Elizabeth was thinking about her siblings too. Her younger brothers still lived locally and had been popping in to see their mother every day or two. She'd written to her sisters a few days ago. Jane and Ann were in London and Fanny in Portsmouth. It didn't take long to get here by train these days but, from what the doctor had said, it might not be time enough. Anthony would be home the day after tomorrow. And then there was William ...

She hadn't even spoken his name, but she knew her mother was thinking of him too when her eyes opened, she tried to sit up and a frown crossed her brow.

"Is the back door open?" Her voice was weak and rasping. "Of course." Elizabeth gently patted her mother's arm. Jane managed a faint smile, laid her head upon the pillow and closed her eyes for the last time.

The Facts

Jane Ibbitson (1822-1896) was my great-great-grandmother.

She was born at Bishopwearmouth, County Durham, the daughter of Anthony Ibbitson (1790-1867) and Frances (née Simpson) and baptised on 15th July. Her father worked in the local glass making industry.

At the time of the 1841 census, William Dempster Murray (1821-1888), a mariner from Lymington, was a lodger in the Simpsons' house. He and Jane were married at St Peter's Monkwearmouth on 16th March 1842 but then set up home in Lymington.

William and Jane had ten children: Elizabeth Georgina, Jane Powell, Anthony John (my great-grandfather), Fanny Ibbitson, William Thomas, David Henry, Sophia Ann (died in infancy), Ann Sophia, Charles and Harry Norton.

Elizabeth married James Andrews in 1867. James came from Yarmouth, Isle of Wight (just four miles across the Solent from Lymington). By 1891 he was a Trinity Pilot, possibly succeeding his father-in-law and/or his own father who had also been a pilot.

Jane (junior) and Sophia were both married in London, Jane to a butcher, Frederick Haydon, and Sophia to a gentleman, Richard Mitchell Beckwith. Fanny had an illegitimate son [See *A Tale of Thomases*]. She later married George Brown and settled in Portsmouth.

The three youngest boys seem to have become carpenters or shipwrights (descriptions vary in the various censuses).

Anthony and William were sailors. Anthony commanded the yacht *Albatross* and lived in Boldre with his wife Eliza (née Bottomer) and family. William, according to family tradition, went to seek his fortune in Australia. He never returned but his mother always left the back door open, just in case.

The Day the Butter Wouldn't Come

Shirley Holms - 1895

Alice brushed her hair, made sure her apron was straight and her room tidy, then went downstairs to report to the housekeeper. "Ah, there you are, Alice. Cook's got a job for you." Alice didn't need to be told what that entailed first thing on a Wednesday morning. Sure enough, the cook sent her to the pantry where four pails of fresh milk stood on the tiled floor.

She picked up the first pail and carefully poured the cream off the top into the butter churn. Likewise with the other three. Then she screwed the cap firmly into place and began turning the wooden handle, humming a little tune to herself as the barrel lurched from end to end and the cream sloshed about inside.

After nearly half an hour the rhythm of churn had not changed. Alice could feel that the cream had not yet separated into butter and buttermilk and her arms were aching. She stopped for a moment and looked out of the window. A large haunch of venison, which was to be the family's Sunday dinner, hung from the yew tree. A solitary magpie had alighted on the rope and was trying to peck at the meat. "One for sorrow" muttered Alice and resumed churning.

Another ten minutes and she had to stop again; her arms were aching so much. The gardener went past with a barrowload of manure and gave her a cheery wave. She smiled and waved back.

"Is that butter ready yet?" "Sorry, Miss Young, it won't come." Cook's ample figure appeared in the doorway. "Then you're not churning hard enough. Get a move on, girl!" Alice sighed; she'd been churning for nearly an hour now and still the butter wouldn't come.

The Facts

Alice Mary House (1877-1967) was my maternal grandmother.

She was the fifth child of Henry and Elizabeth (née Griggs) and grew up at North Weirs in Brockenhurst. They were not well off. Each morning before school Alice and her siblings would walk up to Hincheslea House (about a mile away) where the cook would give them bread and dripping for breakfast. Alice left school at 13 and went into domestic service.

In 1891 she was a general domestic servant in the house of Edward Gibson, the stationmaster at Sway. (Once little more than a hamlet in the parish of Brockenhurst, Sway was a fast-growing village, having acquired its station in 1888 with the extension of the South West Main Line from Brockenhurst to Christchurch and Bournemouth.)

Subsequently she was employed at Shirley Holms and at Rhinefield House, and possibly with the Morant family at Brockenhurst Park, before marrying Thomas William Murray in 1900.

I don't recall her talking much about her time in service, but the one story which came up regularly was the day the butter wouldn't come.

I've possibly made the household at Shirley Holms House sound grander than it actually was. In 1891 the occupier was a retired army officer William Henry Burton, who employed a governess for his three daughters and just three servants, so it was probably much the same when Alice worked there.

But they did like their venison well hung - literally.

The Mariner's Monkey

Portmore, Hampshire – 1920s

Tom slipped the cheese sandwich Alice had made him into the top of his kitbag and pulled the drawstring. He kissed his wife goodbye, shouldered the kitbag and with a cheery "So long!" (it's what he always said whether he was just going down the shore or embarking on a six-month voyage), closed the gate of *The Laurels* and set off up Portmore Hill.

About an hour later he boarded the train at Lymington Town. Another hour and he was alighting at Southampton Central and making his way to the Eastern Docks. He'd been to the Union Castle office a few days earlier and had signed on the *Arundel Castle*, but it wasn't sailing until Monday, so he went back home. Today he arrived in good time, reported to the First Officer, installed himself in the steward's cabin and prepared for the long voyage round the Cape and up the east coast of Africa.

Tom had lost count of the number of times he'd been round the Cape of Good Hope. The first time he'd been a cabin boy aged 13 and was given the customary ducking when they crossed the equator; now he was approaching 50. He began reminiscing about those early voyages on the *Goth* and the *Spartan*. That was in the days when the Union Line was still an independent company. Now those ships were gone; the *Spartan* to the breaker's yard and the *Goth* to Davey Jones' Locker during the war.

As a young single man, he'd been happy to be away for two or three months at a time but when he started courting Alice, the two-week round trip to New York suddenly seemed like a more attractive proposition. So he switched to the north Atlantic route and rather enjoyed the comforts of the modern American vessels, *St Louis* and *St Paul*. He and Alice got married in October 1900 and then he was off to sea again, albeit still crossing the Atlantic, until baby George came along. While the boys were young, he'd made a living locally as a fisherman, and during the War he'd worked with the Royal Engineers at Calshot, but he missed the old routine and developed an urge to see Africa again before he retired.

~~~~~~~~~~~~~~~

Six weeks later the *Arundel Castle* was about to depart from Zanzibar and Tom took the opportunity of a last stroll around Stone Town. He'd always been fascinated by the sheer vibrancy of the place, the colourful markets and the melting pot of cultures. Unlike some of his shipmates, he loved the spicy food. He'd just bought ginger, cinnamon, nutmeg, turmeric and cloves in the market. Alice would be making the Christmas pudding soon and some fresh spices would liven it up. She could make a decent curry too, even though she wouldn't eat it herself. He chuckled at the thought of little Dorothy sitting at his knee while he ate his curry – he'd say "Wan' a bit, Mush?" and she'd take a forkful and screw up her face as if trying hard to enjoy it.

He was walking past the old slave market when suddenly a little furry hand grabbed his earlobe. He turned to find a monkey gazing up at him with big brown eyes. "She like you, suh!" said the grinning youth holding the other end of a tatty piece of rope that was looped around the monkey's neck, "I make you good price for her."

Tom hesitated. It wasn't the first time he'd entertained the idea of buying a monkey. He knew from the dark fur that the animal who was now clinging to his arm and examining the buttons on his shirt, in between glances with those soulful eyes, was a blue monkey. There were two types of monkeys in Zanzibar. The red ones were pretty, but they were delicate creatures and apparently very fussy in their eating habits, but blue monkeys were quite robust; he'd known one or two sailors take them on board ship as pets.

"Found a new friend, Murray?" It was the First Officer who just happened to be passing. "You can take it home if you like. The Master won't mind, as long as you keep it away from the bridge. Only don't hang about. We sail at noon."

That decided it. Tom haggled briefly with the grinning young man, handed over a few coins and the monkey was his. She seemed happy with the deal and clung to his neck as he made his way back to the harbour.

Ginny, as she became known, adapted to life onboard fairly well. For the most part she was confined to Tom's cabin, where he tried with limited success to train her to do her business out of the porthole. Fortunately, the Ship's Cook took a liking to her and would set aside little titbits of fruit and vegetables. She also developed a taste for ship's biscuits. Only once did she escape onto the bridge, but the First Officer, who felt partly responsible for her presence on board, managed to return her to Tom's cabin before the Master noticed.

~~~~~~~~~~~~~~~

On arrival in Southampton, Tom collected his wages and his discharge certificate, noting with relief that his new companion hadn't earned him any black marks, and walked up to the station. Ginny looked slightly nervous as the train hissed and clanked into view, but she held onto Tom's arm. She jumped when the engine let off steam and whimpered for a moment but once they were in the carriage she quietened down and amused herself trying to untie the kitbag. Tom supposed she'd had plenty of time to get used to the ship's engines so maybe the train didn't seem much different. After Beaulieu Road, Ginny sat up and began staring out of the window – they were in the heart of the New Forest now and she hadn't seen any trees for weeks.

Tom got off at Lymington with his kitbag on one shoulder and the monkey on the other, albeit restrained by the leather collar and lead he'd made during the voyage. He turned right out of the station, crossed the Toll Bridge and began to walk up Walhampton Hill. At the sight of the trees, Ginny got excited. She plucked a handful of oak leaves, sniffed cautiously, nibbled one and threw them away in disgust. The soft leaves of a lime tree overhanging a garden fence and cobnuts in the hedgerow proved more to her taste.

Alice was taking in the washing when her husband came through the top gate. She looked askance at the little furry bundle on his shoulder. "Tom Murray! Do you think this house is a zoo? We've already got a dog, a cat and a donkey." She rolled her eyes heavenward. "You'll be up Fareham one of these days!" Ginny just looked at her with those big brown eyes.

~~~~~~~~~~~~~~~

It was a Tuesday morning and Tom was down at the shore doing some work on his boat. Alice was making rissoles when there was a knock at the door. The vicar of South Baddesley stood there with his bicycle. "Good morning, Mrs Murray, I trust you are well?" Alice replied in the affirmative and he continued "Mrs Murray, this may sound odd but" – he paused – "there appears to be a monkey in your apple tree. I was on my way to visit old Mrs Smith at Bull Hill and it threw an apple at me. In fact, it threw three apples at me!" Alice noticed the smudge of apple juice on his bald pate and suppressed a giggle before apologising for Ginny's behaviour and explaining how she came to be there. The vicar graciously accepted the apology and went on his way. From what he knew of Mr Murray, it didn't surprise him in the least that the man now kept a monkey in his house.

It soon transpired that the vicar was not the only traveller on Portmore Hill to be pelted with apples. So when her son Bill came round that afternoon, Alice got him to fetch the ladder from the shed and pick the remaining apples, lest Ginny should use them all for ammunition and they'd have none for the winter. Ginny meanwhile was examining Bill's motorbike – until she touched the exhaust pipe and leapt backwards with a squeal of pain.

As a precaution Alice also picked the little brown pears from the tree behind the shed, even though they weren't quite ripe yet; they would be fine for baking, which was what she always did with them anyway. Ginny wandered off to find Noble, jumped on his back and started pulling his ears. The poor old dog mostly tolerated her, but the cat avoided her and would hiss if she came too close.

As the autumn drew on, Ginny began to get a bit listless. She would hide indoors or in the shed or the privy and would often shiver, which was hardly surprising since she was born just six degrees south of the equator. Alice found the thickest wool she could lay hands on and knitted a little coat which kept her warm and happy during the winter.

The Laurels

The Facts

Thomas William Murray (1873-1960) was my maternal grandfather.

He was born at East Cowes on the Isle of Wight, the eldest child of a ship's captain Anthony John Murray (1849-1901). His mother Eliza was the daughter of Thomas Bottomer, a gardener on the Walhampton estate who originally came from Bramshall in Staffordshire. The family moved to Boldre near Lymington when Tom was quite young.

Following in his father's and grandfather's footsteps, he went to sea at the age of 13 and spent much of his working life as a ship's steward, mainly working on the Cape route out of Southampton. I have some of his discharge certificates for voyages between 1888 and 1901.

He married Alice Mary House (1877-1967), a domestic servant from Brockenhurst, in October 1900. The following year they were living in Captain's Row, Lymington but later moved to Bull Hill in the parish of Boldre. They had three sons, George, William and Frank and, after a gap of 13 years, a daughter, Dorothy (my mother). Around this time, they moved to *The Laurels*, a thatched cottage at the bottom of Portmore Hill.

On one of his voyages (I'm guessing in the early 1920s, but I have no records of his later naval career), Tom brought a monkey back from Zanzibar. Ginny did sit in the apple tree and throw apples at passers-by, and she had a winter coat which Granny knitted for her.

My grandparents lived at *The Laurels* until Tom's death in 1960. I can still picture them sitting in the inglenook next to the little stove where Granny did the cooking (she made wonderful rissoles). There was no electricity, running water or indoor sanitation and water came from two wells in the garden. The privy was a small wooden hut painted in battleship grey; it had a bench seat with a hole in the middle covering a big metal tub, which Tom used to empty behind the hedge, and sheets of old newspaper hung on a hook behind the door. The cottage is still there but modernised beyond recognition and now known as *Heath Cottage*.

When Ginny died, she was stuffed and mounted astride a branch in a glass case along with a polecat, a red squirrel, a curlew and a wood pigeon.

Some of my earliest childhood memories are of Saturday tea at *The Laurels*: hard-boiled seagulls' eggs and wild watercress when they were in season; the soft light and the smell of oil lamps in the winter months – and always Ginny's glassy eyes looking down at me.

In the late 1960s it became apparent that the taxidermist's work was not of the highest standard and sadly Ginny had to be disposed of. However, the polecat took on a new lease of life as a prop for the Hordle Amateur Theatrical Society, starring as "the bloody ferret" in *Sailor Beware*.

Although Ginny's mortal remains have not survived, another piece of taxidermy which used to adorn *The Laurels* is now in my living room: a stuffed loon (or great northern diver) which Granddad shot on the marshes near Lymington. And nearby is an old china dish with a lid, containing a crumbling, but still recognisable, 121-year-old fragment of Tom and Alice's wedding cake.

And yes, they did at some stage own a donkey. It was probably an ancestor of the little band of donkeys that still roam the lanes around Boldre and Brockenhurst.

Postscript 1

You may have noticed that Alice used the expression "up Fareham". Knowle Hospital near Fareham (formerly the Hampshire County Lunatic Asylum) was referred to by Hampshire people of her generation in much the same way as South Londoners referred to "Tooting Bec". Ironically, Alice began to suffer from senile dementia a few years after Tom died and eventually the doctor recommended that she be committed to a psychiatric hospital, so she spent the last few months of her life in Knowle. I hope that in her more lucid moments she never realised where she was – she would have been mortified.

Postscript 2

Thanks to Ginny, I grew up with an image of Zanzibar as an alluringly exotic place. My desire to go there increased over the years and finally came to fruition in 2014. I was not disappointed. It was wonderful to walk the narrow streets of Stone Town and imagine what it might have been like in Granddad's day (probably not a lot different, apart from the absence of the profusion of restaurants). And I saw some of Ginny's distant relatives in the wild – regrettably I couldn't bring one home.

The Rural Economy and the New Fence

Lymington – 1940s

Alice packed her big wicker basket and covered it with a blue gingham cloth. Then she left *The Laurels* by the top gate and walked up the hill. It was a fine spring morning, and she was almost tempted to go down Monument Lane and along the Undershore, but the basket was heavy, so she kept to the main road.

"Morning, Mrs Murray! What can I do for you today?" The butcher beamed broadly, eying Alice's basket. "A pound of rump, if you please." He gesticulated towards a lump of beef on the chopping block. "I've got a nice piece of the point end here, just as you like it." "Fine." said Alice, "I'll just leave my basket here while I go up the High Street."

Twenty minutes later she returned, having been to the haberdashers for some wool and the grocers for curry powder and a few other things you couldn't get in the village shop. "Here you are, Mrs Murray" said the butcher and winked as he handed her the basket. Alice thanked him, placed her purchases on top of the gingham cloth and set off to walk the mile and a half back to Portmore.

She didn't remove the cloth until she got home. In the bottom of the basket, along with the neatly wrapped pound of steak was a handful of coins. And six plump pheasants were now hanging in the butcher's window.

Later that day Tom was walking down Snooks Lane on the way back from his boats when he met Miss Penelope Whittaker. He touched his forelock in a gesture of mock deference. She tried not to smile. "You're a wicked old man, Mr Murray!" She had heard the gunshots yesterday.

~~~~~~~~~~~~~~

"The Shore" – 1950s

It was a Monday morning. For one reason or another, Tom hadn't been down to the shore for the best part of a week, and he was looking forward to spending some time with his boats. Perhaps he'd take the *Bird o' Freedom* across to Yarmouth; he hadn't been out in her for a while. He reached the end of Shotts Lane and turned left onto the foreshore, his boots crunching on the shingle. And then he saw it.

In his absence, the Pylewell Estate had put up a new wire fence, but it was not where the old one had been, it was about six feet closer to the sea! Cursing heartily, Tom turned around and began striding furiously back the way he had come.

Alice was in the garden picking runner beans and knew something was amiss when her husband stormed into the shed muttering under his breath. He gave her the briefest of explanations before picking up his bolt cutters and heading back whence he had just come.

By mid-afternoon the new fence was half a mile of mangled wire laying along the rightful boundary of the estate, above the high-water mark.

The Facts

My maternal grandfather was a champion of the rights of the common man. The foreshore below the high-water mark was common land, not the property of any landowner whose estate happened to back onto it (technically the land between the high and low water marks belongs to the Crown). Pheasants, in his view, belonged to anybody - and he had a rack of shotguns in his shed.

The coastline to the east of the Lymington River estuary is a wild and strangely beautiful landscape. Instead of the sand and shingle beaches which we find at Milford on Sea and Hordle Cliff to the west, there are mudflats covered with a coarse grass known as "spear" (I was told it originated from seed scattered by a shipwreck). A few gnarled and stunted trees line the high-water mark and several tiny streams with wild watercress trickle into the Solent. The stretch between Shotts Lane and Tanners Lane was always known to me as "The Shore" and it was here that my grandfather kept his boats.

The *Bird o' Freedom* was a small petrol-engined cabin cruiser. Tom being a sailor of the old school, there were no "heads" on board - my cousin recalls being told to "stick your arse over the side". There was a rowing boat, painted in the same battleship grey as the privy at *The Laurels*, and I can remember Granddad rowing us around the Lymington River when he was in his early 80s, chewing baccy and periodically ejecting a stream of brown liquid over the gunwale. And there was a punt which was useful for negotiating the mudflats at low tide.

Tom was a thorn in the flesh to the Whittakers of Pylewell Park. They knew perfectly well that he was an occasional poacher, hence Miss Penelope's remark, but they could never catch him. In those days, poaching was not the lucrative criminal activity it often is today. If a man bagged a couple of pheasants for his own table or for his wife to exchange for a piece of steak at the butcher's, nobody minded too much; it was just part of the rural economy*.

But, despite the benefits Granddad received from the estate, the new fence was something he could never tolerate. The foreshore belonged to everyone. And the Whittakers knew it; they didn't dare move the fence again during his lifetime. Sadly, it was moved seaward within six months of his death in 1960 and, as far as I know, remains below the high-water mark to this day.

Postscript

In the 1990s my mother and Miss Penelope would occasionally meet in Lymington Waitrose and exchange a few (friendly) words.

* There were penalties if you were caught though. In 1862 Reuben Medcalf (my great-great-grandfather on the Nunn side), then aged 21, was sentenced to six weeks hard labour for "night poaching at Withersfield".

The Murray Line

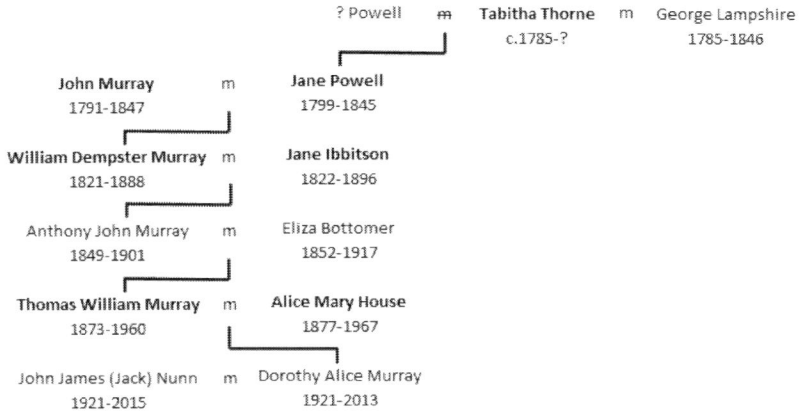

? Powell   m   **Tabitha Thorne**   m   George Lampshire
                c.1785-?   1785-1846

John Murray   m   **Jane Powell**
1791-1847   1799-1845

William Dempster Murray   m   **Jane Ibbitson**
1821-1888   1822-1896

Anthony John Murray   m   Eliza Bottomer
1849-1901   1852-1917

Thomas William Murray   m   **Alice Mary House**
1873-1960   1877-1967

John James (Jack) Nunn   m   Dorothy Alice Murray
1921-2015   1921-2013

The House / Griggs Line

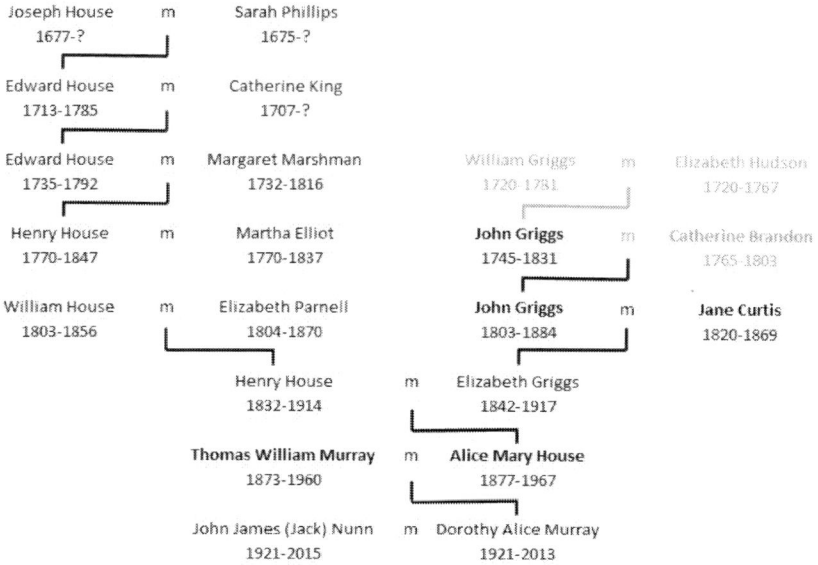

Joseph House   m   Sarah Phillips
1677-?   1675-?

Edward House   m   Catherine King
1713-1785   1707-?

Edward House   m   Margaret Marshman   William Griggs   m   Elizabeth Hudson
1735-1792   1732-1816   1720-1781   1720-1767

Henry House   m   Martha Elliot   **John Griggs**   m   Catherine Brandon
1770-1847   1770-1837   1745-1831   1765-1803

William House   m   Elizabeth Parnell   **John Griggs**   m   **Jane Curtis**
1803-1856   1804-1870   1803-1884   1820-1869

                             Henry House   m   Elizabeth Griggs
                             1832-1914   1842-1917

                    Thomas William Murray   m   **Alice Mary House**
                    1873-1960   1877-1967

                    John James (Jack) Nunn   m   Dorothy Alice Murray
                    1921-2015   1921-2013

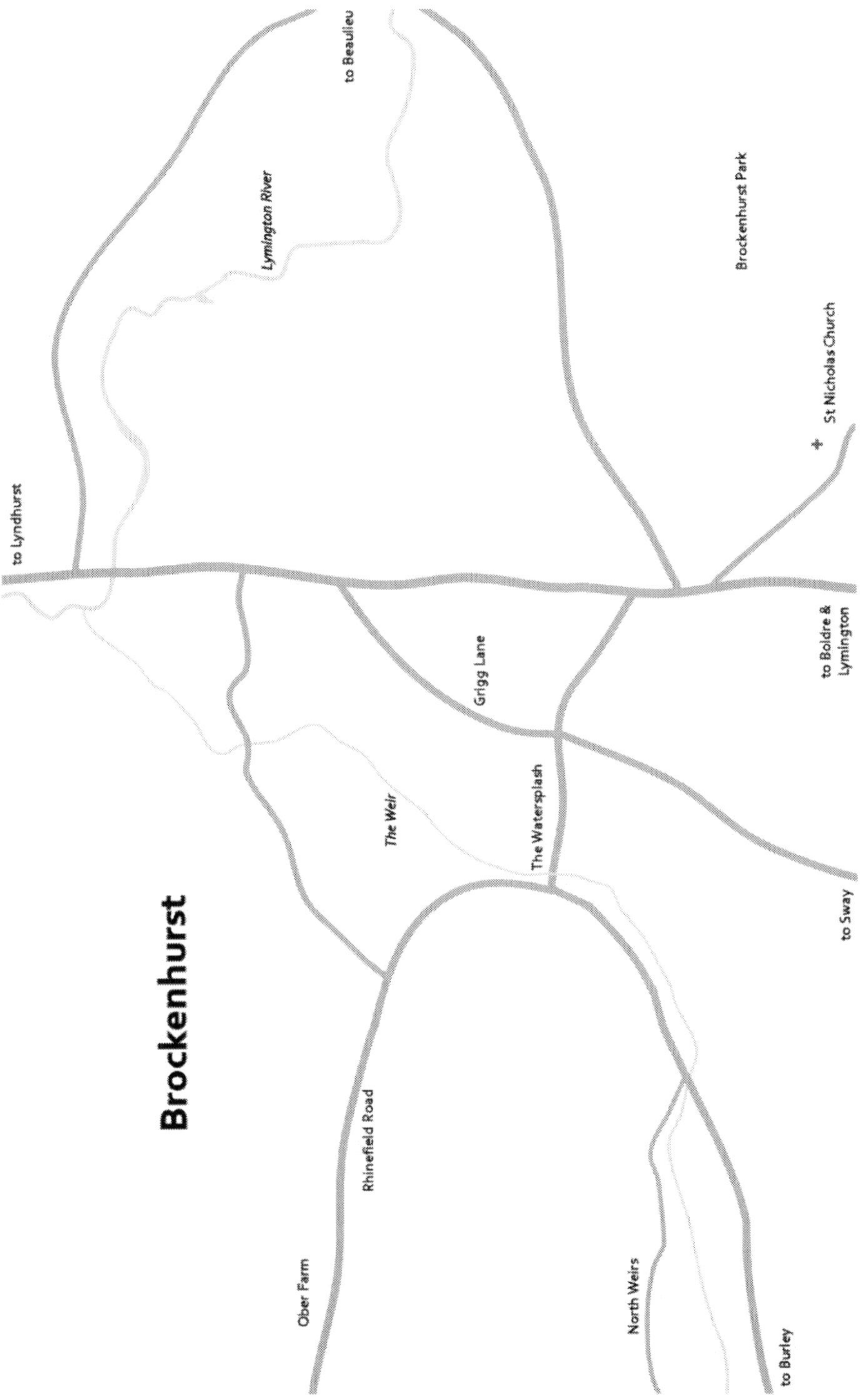

Brockenhurst

Lymington River

to Beaulieu

Brockenhurst Park

St Nicholas Church

to Lyndhurst

to Boldre & Lymington

Grigg Lane

The Weir

The Watersplash

to Sway

Rhinefield Road

Ober Farm

North Weirs

to Burley

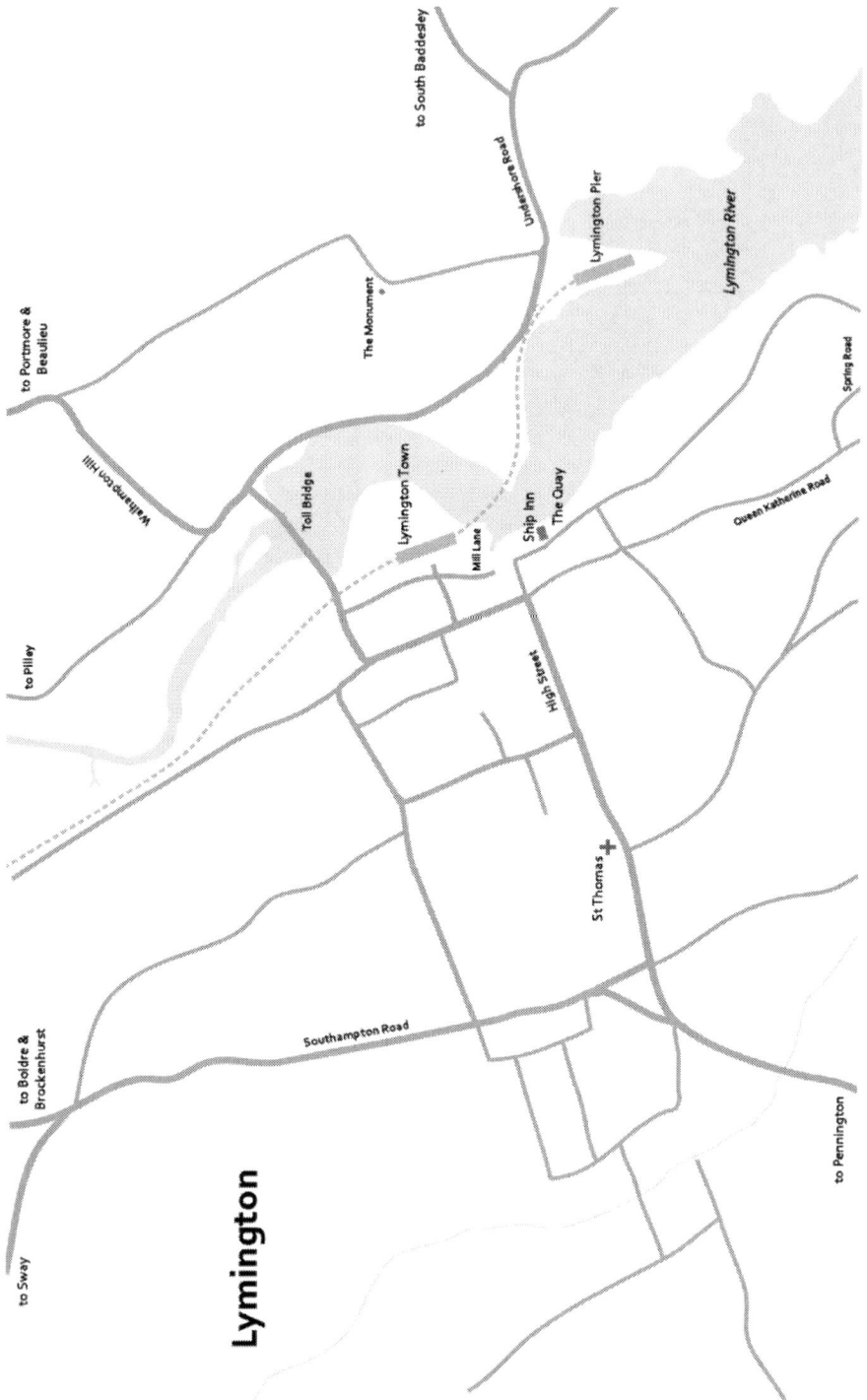

Lymington

to Sway

to Boldre & Brockenhurst

Southampton Road

to Pennington

to Pilley

to Portmore & Beaulieu

Wellington Hill

Toll Bridge

Lymington Town

Mill Lane

Ship Inn

The Quay

St Thomas

High Street

Queen Katherine Road

Spring Road

Undershore Road

to South Baddesley

The Monument

Lymington Pier

Lymington River

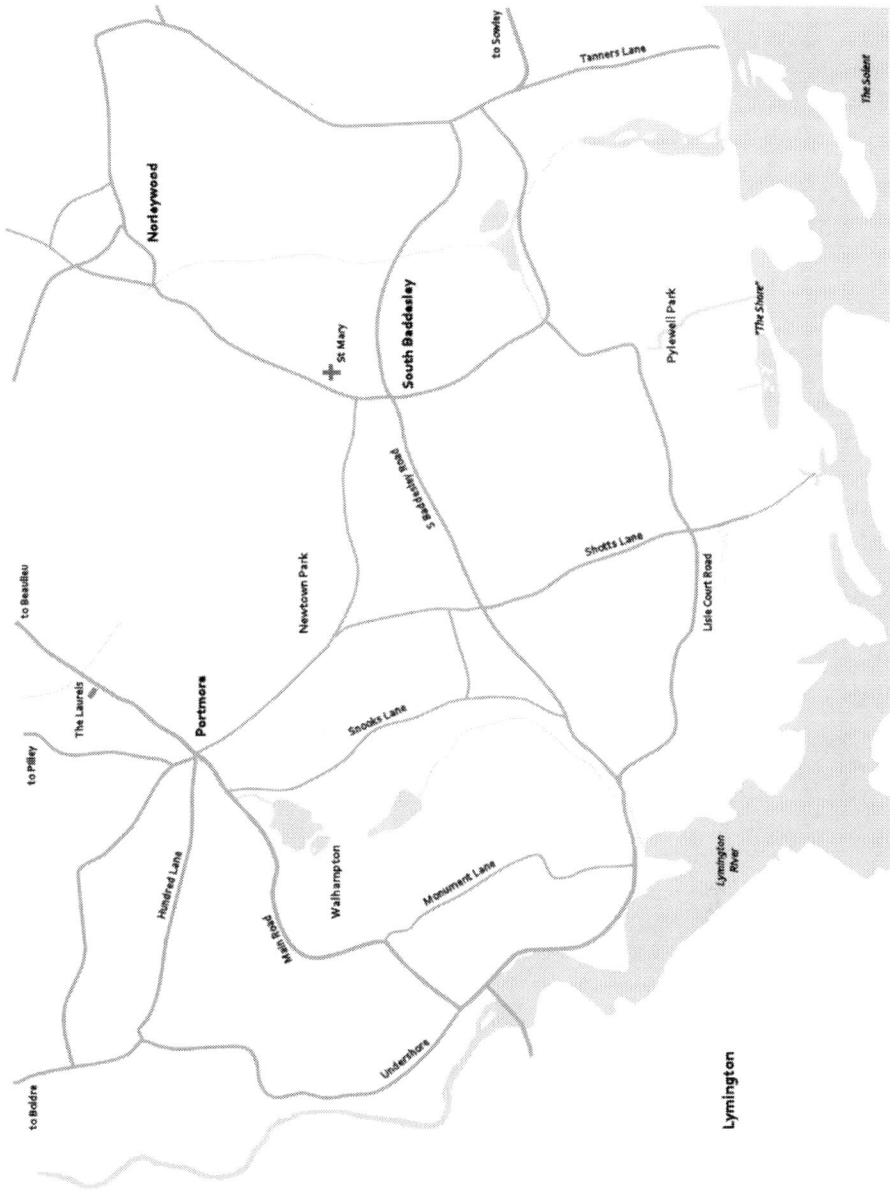

Norleywood

to Sowley

Tanners Lane

The Solent

St Mary

South Baddesley

Pylewell Park

"The Shore"

to Beaulieu

S Baddesley Road

Shotts Lane

Lisle Court Road

Newtown Park

The Laurels

to Pilley

Portmore

Snooks Lane

Walhampton

Hundred Lane

Monument Lane

Main Road

Lymington River

to Boldre

Undershore

Lymington

Dorothy Murray in service (c. 1937)

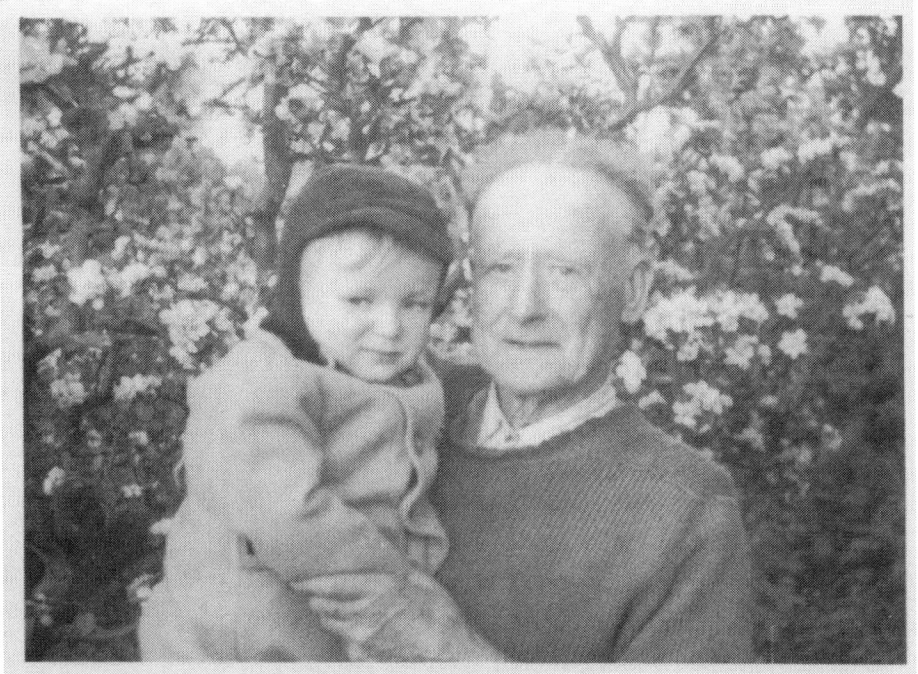
Tom Murray (with the author)

Alice Murray with donkey

The Ship Inn, Lymington

St Nicholas, Brockenhurst

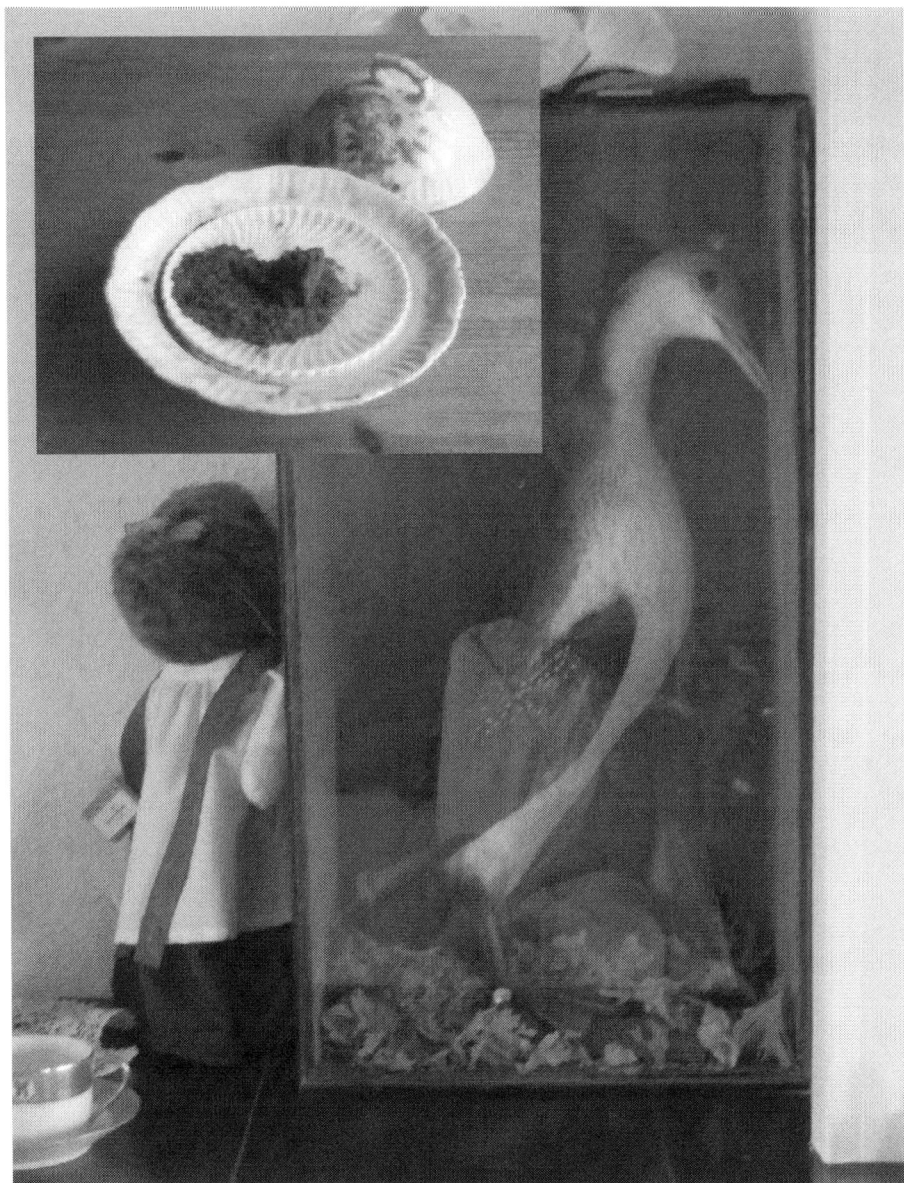

The loon and the wedding cake

Loose Ends

The Beginning of the Line

When I started my research, I knew nothing about the Nunn side beyond my great-grandparents, William and Emma. However, it was fairly straightforward to trace the direct Nunn line back through the census records and then the parish records of St Mary's Haverhill. [I am indebted to Lorraine McPhee, one of the transcribers, who initially provided me with a list of the Nunn entries. I have since acquired records for all the parishes in the Clare Deanery on DVDs provided by the Suffolk Family History Society.]

The earliest relevant entry is the marriage of John Nunn and Mary Willis (my 6th great-grandparents) on 6th February 1722. St Mary's church was burnt down in 1665 so it may be that the records don't go back beyond the late 17th century, but I would have expected to find John's baptism around the 1690s had he been born in the parish.

By convention a wedding normally took place in the bride's parish church, so it seems reasonable to assume that the groom came from a different, but probably local, parish. The most likely candidate is the John Nun (sic), son of Ralph and Martha, baptised at Kedington on 26 March 1696, but for the moment the link is not proven. I'm hoping for a DNA match with one of Ralph and Martha's descendants which would settle the matter.

And what of his wife? In old parish registers there is little consistency in the spelling of surnames and it would seem that Willis was interchangeable with Will(h)ous, Willow(e)s and even Wallis.

By comparing register entries with variants of the surname by the parents' Christian names, I came to the conclusion that Mary was most likely the daughter of Richard and Alice (née Day). They were married at Withersfield in 1691 (when his surname was given as Willis) and Mary was baptised at St Mary's Haverhill on 9th February 1701 (all their children were recorded as Willows or Willow).

Mary died in March 1760. Three months later John married Mary Argent, who died the following April. He lived another ten years.

The Murray Mystery

John Murray was my 3rd-geat grandfather. I've known this since childhood but, in attempting to follow the Murray line further back, I've always hit the proverbial brick wall.

According to family tradition (i.e., my mother told me), he came from Whitley Bay, was the skipper of a collier bringing coal from Tyneside to the south coast, liked Lymington and decide to settle there, becoming landlord of the Ship Inn on the Quay.

What I definitely know:

- He was most likely born around 1791, give or take a year or two.
- On 20th May 1819 he married Jane Powell at St Mary's, Alverstoke (Gosport).
- His son William Dempster Murray was born at Bembridge, IoW, in 1821.
- The 1841 census confirms he was living on Lymington Quay, profession publican, age 49.
- He died at Lymington in 1847.

I have been unable to find any evidence that he was born in Whitley Bay, despite numerous searches on Ancestry and Family Search (that of course isn't conclusive). The nearest match is a John Murray born in Wallsend in 1794. Is Whitley Bay a red herring? Mum's version of family history has been proved wrong before [See *The Wrong House*]. The only definite connection with the north-east is that in 1841 William Dempster was living as a lodger with Anthony and Frances Ibbitson in Sunderland.

It has been suggested that John was born in Malukka, Indonesia – not impossible as the Murrays were a seafaring family – and even that his mother may have been Indonesian, but I've seen no evidence to corroborate the theory. Some of the Murrays had a swarthy complexion and Uncle Frank used to say "We've got a bit of the tar brush in us". However, I'm treating that line of research as low probability.

While the 1841 census does not record place of birth (unlike later censuses), it does have a Y/N column "Born in same county". In John's case the enumerator entered "Y", which could be incorrect but leads me to wonder whether he was born in the Portsmouth area like his wife. There were certainly Murrays in that area, particularly the parish of St Mary Portsea. Maybe he did ship coal from Northumberland but wasn't born there.

I also wonder about the significance of the name Dempster (there was another William Dempster two generations later). Could it have been John's mother or grandmother's maiden name? There were Dempsters in the Portsmouth area.

And another thing. I originally had his name as John William Murray. Where did I get that middle name of William from? Family tradition again? It's just John in the census (but maybe they didn't ask for middle names in 1841) and also in the marriage register.

Might he have been born in Scotland? After all the name Murray is Scottish - there is a Murray tartan and the chief of Clan Murray is the Duke of Atholl. I had always assumed my Murrays had gradually migrated south (i.e., via Northumberland) over the centuries. Might the process have been quicker than that? I found myself drawn (intuition?) to Montrose, a seaport on the east coast. Ancestry searches reveal a lot of Murrays and Dempsters in the area in the 18th century, including John and Elisabeth (née Dempster) Murray who had a son John in 1797 (somewhat outside the optimum timeframe* but feasible). However, that John Murray appears to have been still living in the Montrose area in 1841.

Could the lack of information suggest that he was an orphan or born out of wedlock? His wife Jane was apparently the illegitimate daughter of Tabitha Thorne and an unidentified Mr Powell, so perhaps this was something they had in common. There was a John Murray born to John and Ann of Portsea in 1787 (again outside the optimum timeframe*) and it seems that both parents had died by 1810. Maybe the Dempsters acted as foster parents.

I've spent a lot of time on this and I'm none the wiser. Sometimes I look up at the engraving of Lymington High Street that hangs over my desk and ask the portly gentleman in the top hat (Pilot Murray, aka William Dempster) "Where *did* your Dad come from?".

* I'm assuming a birth year around 1791 from the age of 49 in the 1841 census, but that could well be inaccurate. It was usual in that census to round adult ages to the nearest 5 years (presumably because a lot of people didn't actually know their exact age then).

The Wrong House

If you've ever researched your family history, you'll know how easy it is to make mistakes. Fail to check and re-check your sources or rigorously test your assumptions and you can easily end up barking up the wrong (family) tree.

During the 19th century there were two families called House in Brockenhurst. My maternal grandmother Alice belonged to one of them. Her family lived at North Weirs (near the junction of the now-defunct Brockenhurst to Ringwood railway line). Then there was the other family whom she always referred to as the "Latchmore Houses".

Sometime in the 1960s, my mother happened to mention her mother's family to a local historian, Jude James. He knew a lot about the Houses, being married to one. Mum told him that her grandfather was Robert House, and he told her that Robert was the son of Aaron House and grandson of Jeremiah, who married Ann Payne of Hordle. (We lived in Hordle and I often wondered whether Ann was related to Mrs Payne who cooked and served the school dinners.)

Thus, for over 30 years I believed Aaron and Jeremiah to be my ancestors. I even found Aaron's grave in Brockenhurst churchyard. Mum later acquired some more information showing that Jeremiah was the son of Moses and that the family had originally come from Rockbourne.

But it was all wrong - or rather the vital link was!

I attach no blame whatsoever to the aforementioned historian. He knew his stuff and besides, he was a friend and protégé of my esteemed history teacher, the late Arthur Lloyd. The fact is that Mum got it wrong. She misinformed him.

When I began researching on-line, I discovered that my great-grandfather's name was Henry not Robert. There he was in the 1881 census, living at the Weirs with his wife Elizabeth, the daughter of John and Jane Griggs [See *Granny Griggs's Pig*], and their children, including Alice aged 3. Henry was the son of William House and his family had originally come from Newbury via Kingsclere.

So Aaron, Jeremiah and Moses were the other family, the ones Granny called the Latchmore Houses. It was a little disappointing. I'd rather liked the idea of my ancestors having those splendid biblical names; instead, I ended up with a succession of Williams, Edwards and Henrys. Ah well, *c'est la vie*.

A Tale of Thomases

Some people are assiduous in their research, painstakingly checking and cross-checking their sources, others less so. Some are downright careless, adding an "ancestor" they think they've discovered just because the name is more or less correct and the date is somewhere in the right range. (I suspect this is true of some Americans tracing their English forebears, when they clearly have no knowledge of English geography and little grasp of the limits on social mobility in past centuries.) Looking at other people's family trees which share branches with mine, I've often seen factual errors and misplaced relationships replicated several times –obviously cut-and-pasted with no independent checking of sources.

But sometimes even the "official" sources can be misleading or confusing.

I knew quite a bit about my great-great-grandfather William Dempster Murray [See *Pilot Murray*] before I looked him up in the 1871 census. There he was in Mill Lane, Lymington, listed as head of the household, followed by his wife Jane and six of his ten children: Anthony (my great-grandfather) aged 22, David 15, Thomas 13, Sophia 9, Charles 7, and Harry 6. Then at the bottom of the list is "Thomas ditto - Grandson". The age is not clear but could be a half or three.

I already knew William had two grandsons called Thomas. One was my grandfather, Thomas William Murray – but he wasn't born until 1873. The other was the son of William's eldest daughter Elizabeth, who had married James Andrews in 1867.

However, the very next page of the census lists the Andrews family: James (Head), Elizabeth (Wife) and two sons, James 3 and Thomas 1.

What was going on here? Several possible scenarios came to mind:

1. Granddad was born out of wedlock (his parents married in September 1873) and the family subsequently pretended he was younger than he actually was. Sounds fanciful, I know, but William Dempster Murray was a respected member of the local community and wouldn't have wanted any scandal in his family. Could they have got away with the deception? Possibly – Granddad was quite small in stature (as an adult he only took a size 6 shoe). Incidentally, his mother Eliza Bottomer was at home with her parents in nearby Boldre on census day.

2. One of William's younger daughters had an illegitimate son. If so, I was unable to find any other record of him. He could of course have died soon afterwards.

3. On census day, baby Thomas Andrews was in his grandparents' house. William gave the details of his wife and children and then added "Thomas ditto - Grandson". Meanwhile Mr Andrews gave details of both his sons, although the younger one was at the crucial time with his grandparents a few doors away.

So, what did happen? I was inclined to think the latter, more prosaic, explanation was the correct one. For one thing, Granddad's registered date of birth is 24th October 1873, which is only a month after his parents' wedding, so if they'd already kept quiet about his existence for two and a half years, they'd surely have waited a few more months longer. And if either of scenarios 1 or 2 was the case, would they not have hidden the baby when the census enumerator came round?

The answer when it came to light was far more interesting. It transpired that scenario 2 was the correct one. William's third daughter Fanny Ibbitson Murray did have an illegitimate child in 1868 when she was just 17 - and she called him Thomas William.

In 1872 Fanny married George Brown, a sailor from London about 17 years her senior, and subsequently settled in Portsmouth. But it appears she had already abandoned young Thomas (who was presumably not George's son) to the care of her mother Jane, hence his appearance in William's household in 1871.

Now here's where it gets more interesting. In 1891 Jane was living in Quay Street, Lymington, listed as a widow of independent means (William died in 1888). With her were her two youngest sons, Charles and (Harry) Norton, both in their twenties and working as shipwrights, and a grandchild named as Thomas Brown, aged 24 and working as a saddler. But the 1891 census form has a final column labelled "(1) Deaf & Dumb (2) Blind (3) Lunatic, Imbecile or Idiot" and Thomas is recorded as being "Deaf and dumb from birth".

That set me thinking. My mother had told me about "Dummy" Murray who was a familiar sight in Lymington when she was young. There are references to him (albeit spelt "Dumbie") in *The River Is Within Us*, a book about Lymington characters. He was a deaf-mute who worked at Mew & Langton's depot on Lymington Quay and the only sound he was ever known to articulate was "bugger, bugger, bugger", which he apparently did with monotonous regularity. I had always assumed Dummy must be related to Mum's family in some way. Had I now found him?

I did a bit more searching in the censuses. In 1881 a Thomas Murray from Lymington is listed as a pupil at the Eastern Road Deaf & Dumb Asylum in Brighton. The entries for this establishment run to nearly four pages, starting with the Headmaster William Sleight and Matron Mrs Sarah Sleight, followed by their daughter (Assistant Matron) and a dozen other members of staff and then the inmates, most but not all of whom were children.

In both 1901 and 1911 Thomas was living with his aunt and uncle, Elizabeth and James Andrews, although in the former case his first name is incorrectly given as James, his occupation being saddler or harness maker. Again, the note "Deaf and dumb from birth" occurs in the last column, so there is little doubt about his identity.

So it seems that William Dempster Murray actually had three grandsons called Thomas and one of them was undoubtedly "Dummy" Murray. He died in 1948 at Totton near Southampton.

A Long Shot and a Long Journey?

Sometimes (quite often in fact) in researching our family history we come up against a "brick wall" – an ancestor, or pair of ancestors, whose origins and parentage remain stubbornly elusive, often for years.

And occasionally, from the plethora of data now available on-line, a plausible but improbable and maddeningly unprovable line of enquiry may suggest itself…

The Facts (1)

John Griggs (c. 1745 – 1831) was my 3rd-great-grandfather. His wife's name was Catherine.

The parish registers of Boldre near Lymington, Hampshire, record the following events:
3 June 1798 - Baptism of Ann Griggs, daughter of John & Catherine
9 April 1800 - Burial of Catherine Griggs, daughter of John & Catherine
4 March 1802 - Burial of John Griggs, infant son of John & Catherine
9 January 1803 - Baptism of John Griggs, son of John & Catherine
13 May 1803 - Burial of Catherine Grigg, 38, wife of John of Royden (aged)

I have what appears to be a complete transcript of Phillimore's Hampshire Marriages for Boldre covering the years 1598 to 1812. There is no record of John and Catherine's marriage at Boldre.

In 1817 the Rev'd Henry Comyn carried out a detailed census of the parishes of Boldre and Brockenhurst, where he was Curate. His notebooks have survived and were published in *Comyn's New Forest* (1982) by Jude James. John Griggs senior was living in Brockenhurst as a lodger in the home of Robert Gosney, a shoemaker, and is described as aged. John Griggs junior (my 2nd-great-grandfather) was living at Tythe Barn Farm in Setley (a hamlet between the two villages) as a servant to John Toomer. He later married Jane Curtis and ran a smallholding in Brockenhurst [See *Granny Griggs's Pig*].

The Brockenhurst registers record the burial on 19th March 1831 of "John Grigg aged 86 of the Poor House".

The Facts (2)

Catherine Brandon, the daughter of Robert and Sarah (née Butter), was born in 1765 at Thursford near Fakenham in Norfolk and baptised on 26th May.

On 23rd November 1784 she married John Griggs at Thursford. Her sister Sarah's marriage to William Starling is the next entry in the parish register.

Her husband was almost certainly the John Griggs baptised on 20th October 1745 at Cranworth cum Letton, Norfolk (about 20 miles from Thursford), whose parents were William and Elizabeth (née Hudson).

The Thursford registers record the births of five of their children between 1785 and 1794: Sarah Brandon, Mary, Elizabeth, William and Mark Robert. There are no further references to the family in these registers or those of the neighbouring parish of Hindringham. (Complete facsimiles of parish registers and bishop's transcripts for both parishes – and many others in Norfolk – are available online.)

The Conjecture

Could it be that these two couples are the same John and Catherine Griggs? The dates would seem to match.

Is it possible that sometime between 1794 and 1798 they moved from Thursford to Boldre? If so, why? It was becoming increasingly common in those early days of the Industrial Revolution for people to move from rural areas into towns and cities to obtain work, but why would a couple choose to move from a small village in Norfolk to another village more than 200 miles away in Hampshire?

And how would they have done it? It would have been an arduous journey overland so, if it did happen, it seems more likely that they went by sea from Cromer or Sheringham to Lymington. There was trade between Lymington and ports on the east coast (e.g., bringing coal from Tyneside, as John Murray reputedly did) so this seems quite feasible.

If John and Catherine did make that journey, what became of the five children born in Thursford? None of them appears to have died in infancy or early childhood. I can find no record of any of them in the registers of Boldre or Brockenhurst (although I don't have access to the complete set, apart from the Boldre marriages). Could the children have stayed with their aunt and uncle, the Starlings (who seem to have lost two at least of their own offspring)? Then again, I've seen no conclusive evidence of any of them staying in Norfolk either. (A Mary Anne Griggs married Matthew Pank at Stibbard in 1803. If this was John and Catherine's daughter, she would have been about 16.)

Just suppose all five children died, perhaps in a house fire. That would conceivably provide a motive for the parents to leave the area and start a new life elsewhere. Maybe they were even ostracised by the neighbours as being negligent or somehow responsible for the children's deaths. But surely there would be some record of a funeral even if there were no bodies to bury.

Or maybe they died during the journey – a shipwreck perhaps? However, searching for shipwrecks or maritime disasters finds nothing significant in British coastal waters between the Wash and the Solent during the 1790s.

Might John and Catherine have lived somewhere else between Thursford and Boldre? Possibly, given the four-year gap, but broad searches on theirs and the children's names give no clues.

As I said at the beginning, plausible but improbable and – for the time being at least – unprovable.

Nunn's Yard

Adjoining Camps Road, Haverhill, almost opposite Chauntry Road is a narrow alley. A sign on the wall of what was until a few years ago the Black Horse (alas, it's now a private dwelling) says that this is Nunn's Yard.

I assume it acquired its name from Samuel Nunn who was the landlord of the Black Horse in the 19th century. The 1881 census lists him as an innkeeper aged 58 living in Camps Road. In the previous two censuses he was "innkeeper and baker" or "baker and beer seller" and living in Burton End, and ten years before that he was a gardener. His birthplace is given as Haverhill, but was he a relative of mine?

It appears he was born on 14th June 1821, the son of William and Rebecca, and baptised at St Mary's on 5th August. His parents were presumably the William Nunn and Rebecca Webb who were married on 31st December 1809, but where did William come from? There is no record of his baptism in Haverhill within the likely date range.

Now I have a theory. George Nunn, the youngest son of my 6th great-grandparents John and Mary, had already provided me with an interesting diversion [See *The Link*] but I recently learned a bit more about him, thanks to my cousin Judy. He was married twice: first to Mary Metcalfe in 1758 and then to Ann Stallan in 1773, and lived at Bartlow which is in Cambridgeshire but close to Haverhill (Bartlow was the next station on the former Haverhill to Cambridge railway line).

George had two sons called William, one from each marriage and both baptised in Bartlow. I assume the first one (1762) died young, but might the second one (1775) have married Rebecca Webb in 1809? In which case Samuel Nunn would be my second cousin five times removed.

I'd like to think I have a pub on both sides of the family (the other one being the Ship in Lymington).

The Link

My mother, Dorothy Alice Murray (1921-2013) married my father John James "Jack" Nunn (1921-2015) in 1947. How that came about is a story in itself, so I'll digress for a moment.

Dorothy left school at 14 and went into domestic service with the Cecil family at Passford House near Lymington. From what I've gathered she didn't enjoy it much and the Second World War proved to be a liberating experience for her. She left the Cecils' employ and went to work in the Wellworthy piston ring factory. Around this time, she met a Mrs MacIver who was running a club for the troops in Lymington. Towards the end of the war, "Mrs Mac", as she was commonly known, went to manage a guest house at Lake on the Isle of Wight and Dorothy went with her. She joined Mrs Mac on her next venture too – the Green Hill tea shop in Linton, Cambridgeshire.

Meanwhile Jack, who had also left school at 14 and went to work in a factory which he absolutely hated, had joined the RAF. His eyesight wasn't good enough for aircrew, so they put him in the firefighting department and sent him to work at training camps in Canada where he spent most of the war and had a wonderful time. As a teenager, Jack had joined the Haverhill Wheelers Cycling Club, and on returning home he and his friend Fred Bigmore got the club going again. As well as racing (in those days they thought nothing of cycling the 60-odd miles to Herne Hill on a Saturday morning, racing in the afternoon and cycling home in the evening) they would go on club runs and one of their favourite stopping places was the Green Hill. Dorothy enjoyed cycling too. The rest, as they say, is history.

But that's by the way. Mum had occasionally mentioned that her Aunt Ivy had also married a Mr Nunn and she believed they had been mayor and mayoress of Stoke Newington in London. I often wondered whether there was any connection with Dad's family.

When the census records became available on-line, I decided to try and find out. Ivy Kathleen Murray (1895-1974) was my grandfather Tom's youngest sister. I discovered that she married Ellis Nunn (1894-1968) in 1921 and they did indeed live in Stoke Newington. I don't know where the idea that he was a mayor came from though; I found a list of mayors of the former Borough of Stoke Newington and his name isn't there (nor does he appear to have been mayor of any other north London borough).

However, the most significant thing I discovered is that Ellis was born in

Shudy Camps, Cambridgeshire. I recognised that name immediately. When we used to cycle to my grandparents for our summer holiday, we went through Shudy Camps – it's a little village three or four miles down the road from Haverhill. There just had to be a connection!

Working back though the census records, I soon got to Ellis's great-grandfather Josiah Nunn, also born in Shudy Camps. Then I got stuck, as is often the case when one goes back beyond the early 19th century when the only records were parish records.

That's when the Mormons came to my rescue. The Church of Latter Day Saints has established an enormous database of worldwide genealogical data. The records tend be somewhat disjointed; there are millions of births, marriages and deaths recorded with much duplication and comparatively few links between them. Often they lack vital information like the parish or the date but, with a little perseverance, it's sometimes possible to trace a line through the generations. And so it was that I got back to Josiah's great-grandfather George Nunn.

George's baptism on 9th September 1738 is recorded in the records of the Old Meeting House, Haverhill (a Presbyterian chapel which stood on the site of the later and more substantial church now known as the Old Independent). His parents are named as John and Mary Nunn.

Now I'm reasonably certain that they are same John and Mary (née Willis) who were my 6th-great-grandparents. One curious thing though: their older children, John, Mary and Thomas, were all baptised in St Mary's church, Haverhill. Did they, for whatever reason, decide to become non-conformists sometime between 1734 and 1738? Perhaps they fell out with the vicar?

Anyway, it seems almost certain that Mum's aunt married Dad's 6th cousin.

There's just one final, possible (albeit very tenuous) link in this puzzle. When I started work with the Post Office Data Processing Service in 1971, I was based at Docos House in Commercial Road, London E1 (the building is now a block of flats). There was an elderly lady called Ivy who worked in the staff canteen, and I'm quite sure that one day I heard the canteen manager address her as Mrs Nunn. Our Ivy would have been about 75 at the time and Commercial Road is a few miles from Stoke Newington. But is it just remotely possible that my great-aunt used to serve me my lunch and neither of us realised?

The Link

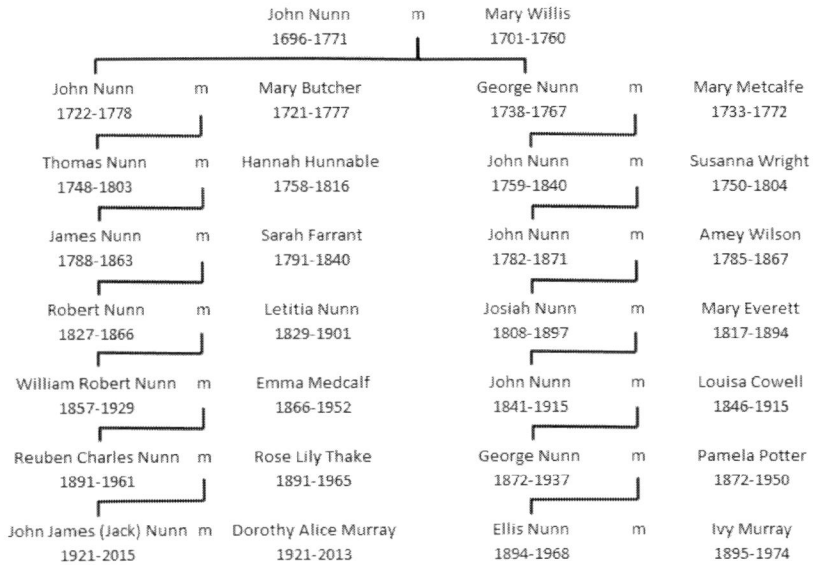

	John Nunn	m	Mary Willis	
	1696-1771		1701-1760	
John Nunn	m	Mary Butcher	George Nunn	m	Mary Metcalfe

John Nunn m Mary Willis
1696-1771 1701-1760

John Nunn m Mary Butcher   George Nunn m Mary Metcalfe
1722-1778 1721-1777   1738-1767 1733-1772

Thomas Nunn m Hannah Hunnable   John Nunn m Susanna Wright
1748-1803 1758-1816   1759-1840 1750-1804

James Nunn m Sarah Farrant   John Nunn m Amey Wilson
1788-1863 1791-1840   1782-1871 1785-1867

Robert Nunn m Letitia Nunn   Josiah Nunn m Mary Everett
1827-1866 1829-1901   1808-1897 1817-1894

William Robert Nunn m Emma Medcalf   John Nunn m Louisa Cowell
1857-1929 1866-1952   1841-1915 1846-1915

Reuben Charles Nunn m Rose Lily Thake   George Nunn m Pamela Potter
1891-1961 1891-1965   1872-1937 1872-1950

John James (Jack) Nunn m Dorothy Alice Murray   Ellis Nunn m Ivy Murray
1921-2015 1921-2013   1894-1968 1895-1974

Miscellaneous

Childhood Memories

Uncle Nort

When I was a child, I saw quite a lot of my maternal grandparents who lived at Portmore, just six miles or thereabouts from our home in Hordle. Normally the whole family would cycle there on a Saturday afternoon and have tea at *The Laurels*, but sometimes my mother would take me and my little brother Geoff by bus during the week. This involved two buses; our local service, Hants & Dorset route 111, would take us to Lymington bus station where we would change to a 112. Mum always sat downstairs but I used to like travelling on the upper deck so I could see out of the big front window and the conductress would give me a ticking off for standing up, sometimes several times during the journey.

The direct route from Lymington to Portmore, via the Toll Bridge and Walhampton Hill, is not far – less than two miles – but the 112 went by a circuitous route via Boldre and Pilley to Bull Hill where we would get off and walk down the hill. As the bus crossed Boldre Bridge (mid-morning on the outward journey), Mum would invariably say "There's Uncle Nort reading his paper". The trouble was, I never knew which house I was meant to be looking at. I don't think I ever did see Uncle Nort.

Harry Norton Murray (1881-1959) was my great uncle.

~~~~~~~~~~~~~~~

Cycling to Haverhill

Visiting my father's parents was an annual event which took place in August. We didn't have a car until 1962 and, if I remember correctly, we did at least once cycle the whole 160 miles in a day, but I think most years we took the train to London (Waterloo) and then cycled to Haverhill.

The mode of cycling varied as I and my brother grew up. When I was very young there was a tandem with a sidecar, but my best memories are of being on the back of Dad's tandem, with an extension chainset or crank shorteners for my little legs, while Geoff rode in a bucket seat on the back of Mum's bike.

We would stop for lunch at the Acme Café in Bishops Stortford, and I recall looking somewhat askance at a green mouldy fork until Dad advised me to sacrifice a chip to clean it. Another year we were somewhere near Saffron Walden when we discovered Geoff no longer had his teddy bear, having decided several miles back that it could run behind.

~~~~~~~~~~~~~~

Reuben's Accordion

I mentioned Reuben's accordion earlier [See *Hokey Pokey*]. It was an old Hohner button accordion or melodeon (B/C tuning). In the 1950s he was still playing it in the shed at 5 Helions Park Grove (I get the impression he wasn't allowed to play it indoors). As a young chorister I would sit at his knee and request my favourite hymn tunes. He only ever played hymn tunes - indeed I don't think that venerable instrument was capable of playing anything else.

In 1962, our first visit after Reuben died, Grandma produced the accordion and I picked it up and played "The church's one foundation" (tune *Aurelia*). My father kept it for many years but eventually its bellows wore out and it probably went to the dump when he moved house.

~~~~~~~~~~~~~~

Dad's Anecdotes

It's a sad fact that when our grandparents, and later our parents, are gone, there are so many things we would like to have asked them but never got round to it. My father used to repeat little anecdotes about people and events which had amused him. Some of these are forever etched on my memory, but I never thought to ask more about the people involved.

Who was Tommy Thickness? Was he a Haverhill man? All I know is that he had a sausage which made a resounding clang when he dropped it on an enamel plate.

And who was the elderly Suffolk gentleman who, when reprimanded by his daughter for pouring his tea into the saucer to cool it, replied "Bun my ol' jars I on't. Sarcer my tea I ull."? Perhaps he was the same character who expressed his disdain for certain places with "Don't think much ol' Bungay, nor ol' Bumpstead."

My father was a very philosophical man; he would pose questions like "Do carrots have souls?". But he also had a knack of observing bizarre little details. One of our churchwardens used to wear very wide and sharply pressed grey flannel trousers; only Dad could have made the observation that when viewed sideways-on the trousers formed a perfect rectangle.

~~~~~~~~~~~~~~

Great Aunt Stella

I never knew most of my paternal grandfather's 14 siblings; I can only recall meeting Ezra (once), Frank, Ruth and Stella.

Stella and Ruth lived in adjacent houses in Withersfield, almost opposite *Lilley Cottage* where they grew up. Stella's husband John Garnett was an artist and a native of Cumberland. A magnificent painting entitled "The Rievers" (cattle rustlers crossing the Solway Firth) hung over the fireplace. He also wound the church clock and once took me up the tower. Having recently become a ringer, I was fascinated by the five bells which had not been rung properly in living memory (sadly they are still derelict nearly 60 years later).

The last time I saw Stella was in 1994, by which time only she and Bryce were left. She showed me the "Family Bible" in which the dates of the 15 were recorded (actually it appears to have originally been David's army issue Bible – presumably he left it behind when he emigrated to New Zealand) and the photo of the six boys in uniform [See *The Sniper's Bullet*]. And she told me a little anecdote. When she was at Withersfield school, another girl said to her "My Mum says 'Don't you have nothing to do with them Nunns, they're funny buggers.'".

I feel I can take some kind of perverse pride in that!

Observations

In the process of genealogical research, certain trends can become apparent – social phenomena which one may not have been aware of before.

Illegitimacy

One thing you discover is that contrary to what some people may think, pre-marital sex wasn't invented in the 1960's. Illegitimate births were not uncommon, even in Victorian times. In baptismal registers the entry "base born" (BB for short) or "bastard" crops up regularly. Often only the mother's name is given, but in some places - particularly it seems in East Anglia - it was not uncommon to record the father's name as well.

There was a good reason for this. The upkeep of a fatherless child became the responsibility of the parish, which provided a powerful incentive for the churchwardens to identify and pursue any man shirking his paternal responsibilities. Fortunately, by the time I became a churchwarden in 1994 the duties had become somewhat less onerous!

Sometimes the baptism of a first child took place after the wedding, but the birth clearly preceded it. In even more cases (I haven't worked out the statistics but I'm estimating at least 50% in my own family) the gap between the marriage and the birth was rather less than nine months.

Illiteracy

Another thing which quickly becomes apparent is the effect of the Elementary Education Act 1870, which made education compulsory for children aged 5 to 13 (although it took some years to achieve anything like 100% compliance).

From the dark ages to the early 19th century the ability to read and write was largely confined to the aristocracy, clerics, lawyers and academics and maybe merchants and officers in the armed forces. With the coming of the industrial revolution, literacy extended to the new middle classes but the average farm labourer, mill worker or housewife was still illiterate and uneducated. The extent of illiteracy can be seen from marriage registers, where the bride, groom and two witnesses were required to sign or, if they were unable, make their "mark".

It came as a surprise to me to discover that most of my great-great-grandparents (the generation getting married in the mid-19th century) were illiterate (as evident by "his/her mark" on the marriage certificate). By the time the next generation got married we have 100% literacy.

As an aside, I initially found the practice of making one's mark puzzling. Surely even illiterate people could learn to write their own name. But it later occurred to me that learning to write is not just an intellectual exercise; it involves acquiring motor functions and a particular dexterity which are not part of basic human activity, and the effort required is probably not worthwhile merely for the purpose of being able to produce a signature. This in turn caused me to wonder whether today's children who have grown up using computers and smartphones have difficulty with handwriting or even signing their names. My own handwriting, which was never neat, has deteriorated noticeably in the past two or three decades, as I only ever use it for scribbled notes.

Recycling Names

Forenames or Christian names often recur in successive generations of a family. But it was also common for them to be recycled within a generation. If a child died, the same name would be given to the next child of the same gender to be born.

I suspect many people nowadays would find this practice distasteful, but we must remember that in the past infant and child mortality was a fact of life, not a rare and unbearably tragic occurrence calling for massive outpourings of grief. It was not at all unusual for a family to lose a child or two. The fact that all 15 of my great-grandparents' children survived to adulthood and subsequently lived to 70 plus – now that was unusual!

Localised Surnames

While looking through parish records of Boldre and Brockenhurst in search of maternal ancestors, I couldn't help noticing certain names kept cropping up: Drodge, Jenvey, Kitcher and Linney. Those names were familiar to me in my childhood, growing up as I did in that area. But I have seldom if ever encountered them since and indeed had almost forgotten them.

Some surnames are ubiquitous and some are concentrated in particular regions (there are an awful lot of Nunns in East Anglia and comparatively few of us elsewhere), but it rather surprised me that even in this day and age names could be so localised.

Acknowledgements

Gill, for proof-reading and ongoing love and support.

My second cousin, Judy, whose meticulous research has frequently corroborated, corrected and inspired mine. Also Jackie and Julianne for their insights.

.

Printed in Great Britain
by Amazon